HIS BIG
OPPORTUNITY

AMY LE FEUVRE

1st WORLD
LIBRARY
Literary Society

His Big Opportunity

Amy Le Feuvre

© 1st World Library, 2009
PO Box 2211
Fairfield, IA 52556
www.1stworldlibrary.com
First Edition

LCCN: 2009923339

Softcover ISBN: 978-1-4218-8806-4
Hardcover ISBN: 978-1-4218-8905-4
eBook ISBN: 978-1-4218-8707-4

Purchase *"His Big Opportunity"*
as a traditional bound book at:
www.1stWorldLibrary.com/purchase.asp?ISBN=978-1-4218-8806-4

1st World Library is a literary, educational organization
dedicated to:

- Creating a free internet library of downloadable ebooks

- Hosting writing competitions and offering book
  publishing scholarships.

Interested in more 1st World Library books?
contact: literacy@1stworldlibrary.com
Check us out at: www.1stworldlibrary.com

1ˢᵗ World Library Literary Society

Giving Back to the World

"If you want to work on the core problem, it's early school literacy."

- James Barksdale, former CEO of Netscape

"No skill is more crucial to the future of a child, or to a democratic and prosperous society, than literacy."

- Los Angeles Times

"Literacy... means far more than learning how to read and write... The aim is to transmit... knowledge and promote social participation."

- UNESCO

"Literacy is not a luxury, it is a right and a responsibility. If our world is to meet the challenges of the twenty-first century we must harness the energy and creativity of all our citizens."

- President Bill Clinton

"Parents should be encouraged to read to their children, and teachers should be equipped with all available techniques for teaching literacy, so the varying needs and capacities of individual kids can be taken into account."

- Hugh Mackay

CONTENTS

I

ON THE GARDEN WALL

They were sitting astride on the top of the old garden wall. Below them on the one side stretched a sweet old-fashioned English garden lying in the blaze of an August sun. In the distance, peeping from behind a wealth of creepers and ivy was the old stone house. It was at an hour in the afternoon when everything seemed to be at a standstill: two or three dogs lay on the soft green lawn fast asleep, an old gardener smoking his pipe and sitting on the edge of a wheelbarrow seemed following their example; and birds and insects only kept up a monotonous and drowsy dirge.

But the two little figures clad in white cricketting flannels, were full of life and motion as they kept up an eager and animated conversation on their lofty seat.

"You see, Dudley, if nothing happens, we will make it happen!"

"Then it isn't an opportunity."

"Yes it is. Why if those old fellows in olden times hadn't ridden off to look for adventures they would never have found them at home."

"But an opportunity isn't an adventure."

"Yes, it is, you stupid! An adventure is something that happens, and so is an opportunity."

The little speaker who announced this logic so dogmatically, was a slim delicate boy with white face, and large brown eyes, and a crop of dark unruly curls that had a trick of defying the hair cutter's skill, and of growing so erratically that "Master Roy's head," was pronounced quite unmanageable.

He was not a pretty boy, and was in delicate health, constantly subject to attacks of bronchitis and asthma, yet his spirit was undaunted, and as his old nurse often said, "his soul was too strong for his body."

Dudley, his little cousin, who sat facing him, on the contrary, was a true specimen of a handsome English boy. Chestnut hair and bright blue eyes, rosy cheeks, and an upright sturdy carriage, did much to commend him to every one's favor: yet for force of character and intellect he came far behind Roy.

He sat now pondering Roy's words, and kicking his heels against the wall, whilst his eyes roved over the road on the outside of the garden and away to a dark pine wood opposite.

"Here's one coming then," he said, suddenly; "now you'll have to use it."

"Who? What? Where?"

"It's a man; a tramp, a traveller or a highwayman, and he may be all the lot together! It's an opportunity, isn't it?"

Roy looked down the narrow lane outside the wall, and saw the figure of a man approaching. His face lit up with eager resolve.

"He's a stranger, Dudley; he doesn't belong to the village; we'll ask him who he is."

"Hulloo, you fellow," shouted Dudley in his shrill boyish treble; "where do you come from? You don't belong to this part."

The man looked up at the boys curiously.

"And who may ye be, a-wall climbin' and a breakin' over in folks' gardens to steal their fruit?"

"Don't you cheek us," said Roy, throwing his head up, and putting on his most autocratic air; "this is our garden and our wall, and the road you're walking on is our private road!"

"Then don't you take to insulting passers-by, or it will be the worse for ye!" retorted the man.

The boys were silent.

"I'm sure he isn't an opportunity," whispered Dudley.

But Roy would not be disconcerted.

"Look here," he said, adopting a conciliatory tone; "we're looking out for an opportunity to do some one some good, and then you came along, that's why we spoke to you.

Now just tell us if we can do it to you."

"Yes," Dudley struck in: "you seem rather down, do you want anything that we can give you?"

The man glanced up at them to see if this was boyish impudence, but the faces bending down were earnest and grave enough, and he said with a short laugh,—

"Oh, I reckon there be just a few things I'm in want of; but as to your givin' of them to me that be quite a different matter. Don't suppose ye carry about jobs ready to hand in yer pockets, nor yet my set of tools in pawn, nor yet a pint o' beer and a good hunk of bread and meat for a starvin' feller! May be ye could tell me the way to the nearest pub, and stand me a drink there!"

Roy thrust his hand immediately into his pocket, and pulled out amongst a confused mass of boys' treasures a sixpence.

"I'll give you this if it will do you good," he said, holding it up proudly. "I've kept it a whole two days without spending it. It will give you some beer and bread and cheese, I expect. Is there anything else we can do for you?"

"If you go to Mr. Selby, the rector, he'll put you in the way of work," shouted out Dudley, as the man catching the sixpence flung down to him slouched off with muttered thanks.

"No parsons for me," was the rejoinder.

The boys watched his figure disappear down the road, and then Roy said reflectively,—

"Too many opportunities like that would empty our pockets."

"And I wonder if it will really do him good," said Dudley; then glancing over into the garden, he added: "Here comes Aunt Judy, she's calling us."

Down the winding gravel path came their aunt; a strikingly handsome woman. She looked up at her little nephews and laughed when she came to the wall.

"Oh, you imps, do you know I've been hunting for you everywhere! You will have a fall like Humpty Dumpty if you choose such high perches. Now what comfort can you find, may I ask, in such a blazing breakneck seat? Do you find broken bottles a soft cushion?"

"We've cleared those rotten things away here," said Dudley, preparing to clamber down; "it's our watch tower, and we've a first-rate view, you just come up and see!"

"Thank you, I would rather not attempt the climb. What have you been talking about? Jonathan looks as grave as a judge."

Roy looked down at his aunt without moving.

"If you won't laugh or tell granny, we'll tell you, because you never split if you say you won't."

"All right, I promise."

"Well, you see, this morning Mr. Selby gave us this for our copy: 'As ye have opportunity do good unto all men,' and he told us of a King somebody—I forget who—who used to write down at the end of each day on a slate,—if he hadn't done any good to any one,—'I've lost a day.' We thought it would be a good plan to start this afternoon and see what we could do. We tried on old Hal first, but he didn't seem to like it. He was uncovering some of the frames, and so we went and uncovered all of them, and then he said we had spoilt some of his seedlings, and nearly went into a fit with rage. I turned the hose on him to cool him down. He is asleep in the wheelbarrow now; we can see him from here. We really came up here to get out of his way, his language was awful!"

"Come down, you monkey. I can't carry on a conversation with you so far above me. Softly now. Bless the boys, how they can stick their toes into such a wall is past my comprehension! Granny wants to see you before your tea, so come along. And who else has been benefited by your good deeds?"

They were walking toward the house by this time, each boy hanging on to one of her arms. It was easy to see the affection between them.

Dudley eagerly poured out the story of the tramp, and Miss Bertram listened sympathetically.

"Never send a man to a public house, boys—and never give him money for beer. Perhaps he may have come down in the world through love of it. You know I am always ready to give any one a relief ticket. That's the best way to help such cases."

"Yes, but that would be your doing not ours."

"Money is a difficult way of helping," said Miss Bertram; "don't get into the habit of thinking money is the only thing that will do people good. It too often does them harm."

"Oh, I say! that's hard lines on me, when my last sixpence has gone, and I was going to get a stunning ball old Principle has in his shop!"

Miss Bertram laughed at Roy's woe-begone little face.

"Never mind," she said, consolingly; "your intentions were good, and you must buy your experience by mistakes as you go through life. Now go into granny softly, both of you, and talk nicely to her. She will be one person you can do good to, by brightening her up a little."

Dudley made a grimace at Roy; but both boys entered the house, and crept into a cool half-darkened drawing-room on tiptoe, with hushed voices and sober demeanor. A stern looking old lady sat upright in her easy chair, knitting busily. She greeted the boys rather coldly.

"What have you been doing with yourselves? I sent for you some time ago. Do you not remember that I like you to come to me every afternoon about this hour?"

"Yes, granny," said Roy, climbing into an easy chair opposite her; "we were coming only we didn't know it was so late: we were busy talking."

"Boys' chatter ought not to come before a grandmother's wishes."

There was silence; then Dudley struck in boldly:

"We were talking about good things, granny. It wasn't chatter. Roy and I are going to look out for opportunities every day of our lives. Do you think an opportunity is the same as an adventure? I don't think you have adventures of doing good, do you?"

"Yes," asserted Roy, bobbing up and down in his chair excitedly; "King Arthur and his knights did always. They never rode through a wood without having an adventure, and it was always doing good, wasn't it, granny?"

Conversation never slackened when the boys were present, and Mrs. Bertram, though shrinking at all times from their high spirits and love of fun, yet looked forward every day to their short visit. She was a confirmed invalid, and rarely left the house, and her daughter Julia in consequence took her place as mistress over the house-hold.

Three years before, Roy and Dudley arrived within a month of each other, to find a home with their grand-mother. Roy, whose proper name was Fitzroy, came from Canada, both his parents having died out there. Dudley's father had died when he was a baby, but his mother had married again in India; and upon her death which occurred not long after, his stepfather had sent him home to his grandmother. From the first day that they met, the boys were sworn friends; and their aunt dubbed them "David" and "Jonathan" after having been an unseen witness of a very solemn vow transacted between them under the shadow of the pines, only a week after their meeting.

Roy's delicate health was a cause of great anxiety to his grandmother, and if it had not been for Miss Bertram's wise tact and judgment, he would have been imprisoned in one room and swathed in cotton wool most of the year round. He had the advantage of having an old nurse who had brought him up from his birth, and had come from

Canada with him; and she was as vigilant and experienced in managing his ailments as could be desired. Poor little Roy, with his uncertain health, was heir to a very large property of his father's not far away; and the responsibilities awaiting him, and the knowledge that he would have so much power in his hands, perhaps had the effect of making him weigh life more seriously than would most boys of his age.

Later on after their visit to their grandmother was over, and tea had been finished in the nursery, he wandered into his own little room, and leaning out of his window, looked up into the clear sky above.

"I feel so small," was his wistful thought, "and heaven is so big; but I'll do something big enough to get, 'Well done good and faithful servant,' said to me when I die, I hope. And I'll try every day till I do it!"

II

A SONG

"Come here, boys. I have had some new music from town, and here is a song that you will like to listen to, I expect."

It was Miss Bertram who spoke, and her appearance in the nursery just saved a free fight. Wet afternoons were always a sore trial to the boys: their mornings were generally spent at the Rectory under Mr. Selby's tuition, but their afternoons were their own, and it was hard to be kept within four walls, and expected to make no sound to disturb their grandmother's afternoon nap.

The old nurse was nodding in her chair, and her charges with jackets off and rolled up shirt sleeves were advancing toward each other on tiptoe, and muttering their threats in wrathful whispers.

"I'll show you I'm no coddle!"

"And I'll show you I'm no lazy lubber!"

At the sound of their aunt's voice they stopped; and each picked up his jacket with some confusion, Dudley saying contentedly, "All right, old fellow, pax now, and we'll finish it up to-morrow."

"Aunt Judy, do let us come into the drawing-room then, and hear you sing; we're sick of this old nursery, we're too big to be kept here."

Roy spoke scornfully, but his aunt shook her head at him:

"Do you know this is the room I love best in the house? Your father and I used it till we were double your age, and no place ever came up to it in our estimation. Don't be little prigs and think yourselves men before you're boys!"

"Why, Aunt Judy, we've been boys ever since we were born!"

"I look upon you as infants now," retorted Miss Bertram, laughing. "Come along—tiptoe past granny's room, please, and no racing downstairs."

"We'll slide down the rails instead, we always do when granny is asleep."

"Not when I am with you, thank you."

A few minutes afterward, and the boys were standing on either side of the piano listening with delight to the song that has stirred so many boyish hearts:

"'Tis a story, what a story, tho' it never made a noise
Of cherub-headed Jake and Jim, two little drummer boys
Of all the wildest scamps that e'er provoked a sergeant's eye,

They were first in every wickedness, but one thing
could not lie,
And they longed to face the music, when the tidings
from afar
Brought the news of wild disaster in a wild and savage
war.
Said the Colonel, 'How can babies of battle bear the
brunt?'
Said the little orphan rascals, 'please Sir, take us to the
front!
And we'll play to the men in the far-off land,
When their eyes for home are dim;
If the Indians come, they shall hear our drum
In the van where the fight is grim.
Our lads we know, to the death will go,
If they're led by Jake and Jim.'

"In the battle, 'mid the rattle, and the deadly hail of
lead,
The two were in their glory—What did they know of
dread?
And fierce the heathen cry arose across the Indian
plain,
And 'twas Home, for the bravest there would never be
again,
The raw recruits were restless, and they counted not
the cost,
And the Colonel shouted, 'Steady lads, stand fast, or
else we're lost.'
A rush! 'twas like an avalanche! a clash of steel and
red! A shock like mountain thunder, then the reg'ment
turned and fled.
'Give me the drum, take the fife,' said Jake,
'And with all your might and main,
Play the old step now, for the reg'ment's sake
As they scatter along the plain.

We'll play them up to the front once more,
Tho' we never come back again.'

"Then might the world have seen two little dots in red,
Facing the foe, when the rest had turned and fled!
So young, so brave and gay, while others held their
breath,
They played ev'ry inch of the way to meet their death;
And *then* at last the reg'ment turned, for vengeance
ev'ry man
To save the lads they turned and fought as only
demons can;
They swept the foe before them across the mountain
rim,
But victory that day could never bring back Jake or
Jim.
And they silently stood where the children fell,
Not a word of triumph said,
For they knew who had led as they bowed each head,
And looked at the quiet dead;
That the fight was won, and the reg'ment saved,
By those two little dots in red."

Miss Bertram stole a glance at the boys' faces as she finished singing.

With a wriggle and a twist Dudley turned his back upon her; but not before she had seen the blue eyes swimming with tears, and heard a choking sob being hastily swallowed. Roy stood erect, his little face quivering with emotion, and his usually pale cheek flushed a deep crimson, whilst his small determined mouth and chin looked more resolute and daring than ever. His hands thrust deep in the pockets of his knickerbockers he looked straight before him and repeated with emphasis,

"They played every inch of the way to meet their death!"

"Regular little heroes, weren't they?" said Miss Bertram.

"Rather," came from Roy's lips, and then without another word he ran out of the room.

"Do you like it, David?" Miss Bertram asked, touching Dudley lightly on the shoulder.

"No—I—don't—it makes a fellow in a blue funk." And two fists were hastily brushed across the eyes.

"Shall I sing you something more cheerful?"

"No, thanks, not to-night, I think I'll go to Roy."

And Dudley, too, made his exit, leaving his aunt touched and amused at the effect of the song.

An hour after the rain had ceased, and the sun was shining out. Down the village street walked the two boys enjoying their freedom more soberly than was their wont.

"We must, we must, we *must* be heroes, Dudley!"

"Yes, if we get a chance."

"But why shouldn't we have it as well as those two boys. I wonder sometimes what God meant us to do when He made us! And I'm not going to be in the dumps because I'm not very strong. For look at Nelson: old Selby told us he was always very seedy and shaky, always ill; and not being big in body doesn't matter, for Nelson was a little man and so was Napoleon, and lots of the great men have been short and stumpy and hideous! I mean to do

Amy Le Feuvre

something before I die, if only an opportunity will come! Do you remember the story of the little chap in Holland, who put his hand in the hole in the sand bank, and kept the whole ocean from coming in and washing away hundreds of towns and villages? If I could only do a thing like that, something that would do good to millions of people; something that would be worth living for! If I could save somebody's life from fire, or drowning, or some kind of danger! Don't you long for something of that sort, eh?"

"I don't know that I do," was the slow response; "but I should like you to get a chance of it if you want it so much."

"Oh, wasn't it splendid of those two little chaps—a whole regiment! And only those two who didn't run away! I think I could stand fire like that, couldn't you?"

"I would with you."

"But I don't expect I'll ever go into the army." This in sorrowful tones.

"Why not?"

"Oh, they'd never have me. I'm too thin round the chest; nurse says I'm like a bag of bones, and I wouldn't make a smart soldier. Now you'd be a splendid one, no one could be ashamed of you."

"Well, I won't go without you."

"But I'll do something worth living for," repeated Roy, tossing up his head and giving a stamp as he spoke; "and I'll seize the first opportunity that comes."

Dudley was silent. They had now reached the low stone bridge over the river, a favorite resort amongst all the village boys for fishing; and quite a little group of them were collected there. Roy and Dudley were welcomed eagerly as though perhaps at times they were inclined to assume patronizing and masterful airs; yet their extreme generosity and love for all country sport made them general favorites with the villagers.

Roy was soon in the midst of an eager discussion about the best bait for trout; and was presently startled by a heavy splash over the bridge. Looking up, to his amazement, he saw Dudley struggling in the water.

"Help, Roy, I'm drowning!"

Both boys were capital swimmers, but Roy saw that Dudley seemed incapable of keeping himself up, and in one second he threw off his jacket, and dived head foremost off the bridge to the rescue. The current of the river was strong here, for a mill wheel was only a short distance off; and it was hard work to swim safely ashore. Roy accomplished it successfully amidst the cheers of the admiring group on the bridge; and when once on dry ground again, neither of the boys seemed the worse for the wetting. In the hubbub that ensued Dubley was not questioned as to the cause of the accident; but it appeared that his feet had got entangled in some string and netting that one of the boys had brought with him to the bridge, and it was this that had prevented him from swimming.

"It's awfully nice that I had the chance of helping you," said Roy, as the two boys were running home as fast as they could to change their wet clothes; "I didn't hurt you in the water, did I? I believe I gave a pretty good tug to your hair, I was awfully glad you hadn't had your hair cut lately."

"You've saved my life," said Dudley, staring at Roy with a peculiar gravity; "if you hadn't dashed over to me, I should have been sucked down by that old wheel, and should have been a dead man by this time. You've done to-day what you were longing to do."

"Yes, but I tell you I felt awfully squeamish when I saw you in the water and thought I might be too late."

As they neared the house, Roy's pace slackened.

"Go on, Dudley, and leave me, I can't get on, I believe that horrid old asthma is coming on, I'll follow slowly."

"I'm not quite such a cad," was Dudley's retort, and then hoisting Roy up on his back, as if that mode of proceeding was quite a usual occurrence, he made his way into the house.

They crept up to their bedrooms and changed their wet clothes before they showed themselves to any one. Then Dudley waxed eloquent for the occasion, and the story was told in drawing-room and servants' hall, till every one was loud in their praises of the little rescuer.

"He looks too small to have done it," said Miss Bertram, smiling; for though Roy was Dudley's senior by two months, he was a good head shorter.

Roy got rather impatient under this adulation.

"Oh, shut up, Dudley, don't be such an ass, as if I could have done anything else!"

An hour after, and Roy was sitting up in bed speechless and panting, with the bronchitis kettle in full play, and nurse trying vainly to battle with one of his worst bronchial attacks.

"I say "—he gasped at last; "do you think—I'm going to die—this time?"

"Surely no, my pet. It's more asthma than bronchitis; I'll pull you round, please God."

Midnight came, and when nurse left the room for a minute she found a small figure crouched down outside the door.

It was Dudley.

"Oh, nurse, he's very bad, isn't he? Is he going to die? What shall I do! I shall be his murderer, I've killed him!"

Dudley's eyes were wild with terror, and nurse tried to soothe him.

"Don't talk nonsense, but go to bed; he'll be better in the morning, I hope. It's just the wet, and the strain of it that's done it. There's none to blame. You couldn't help it, and he's been as bad as this before and pulled through. Go to bed, laddie, and ask God to make him better."

Dudley crept back to bed, and flung himself down on his pillows with a fit of bitter weeping.

"She says I couldn't help it; oh, God, make him better, make him better, do forgive me! I never thought of this!"

III

MAKING AN OPPORTUNITY

It was two days before Dudley was allowed to see the little invalid. The doctor had been in constant attendance; but all danger was over now, and Roy as usual was rapidly picking up his strength again.

"His constitution has wonderful rallying powers," the old doctor said; "he is like a bit of india rubber!"

It seemed to Dudley that Roy's face had got wonderfully white and small; and there was a weary worn look in his eyes, as he turned round to greet him.

"Now sit down and talk to him, but don't let him do the talking," was nurse's advice as she left the boys together.

Dudley sat down by the bed, and squeezed hold of the little hand held out to him.

"I'm so sorry, old chap," he said, nervously; "do you feel really better? I've been so miserable."

"I'm first-rate now," was the cheerful response; "it's awfully nice getting your breath back again; it's only made me feel a little tired, that's all!"

"It was all me!"

"Why that has been my comfort," said Roy, with shining eyes; "I felt when I was very bad, that if I died, I might have lived for something. It would have been lovely to die for you, Dudley—at least you know to have got myself ill from that reason; it's so very tame when I get bad from nothing at all; but I'm well again now, so I know God is letting me live to do something else!"

"I was the one that ought to have been made ill to punish me," blurted out Dudley, and then he was silent.

Roy's eyes rested on his flushed face with some wonder.

"It wasn't wicked of you to fall into the river; you couldn't help it."

A crimson flush crept over Dudley's face up to the very roots of his hair; he picked the fringe of the counterpane restlessly between his fingers, and kicked his heels against the legs of his chair. Silence again: Roy looked steadily at him; and then an expression of astonishment and bewilderment flitted across his face, followed by one of strange, conviction.

"Dudley, look at me."

Roy's tone was peremptory, but Dudley never moved, until the command was given in a sharper tone. Then he raised his head, but his blue eyes had a guilty harassed look in them, and he dropped them quickly again.

"It's no good; I've found you out. Did you tie up your feet

Amy Le Feuvre

like that yourself?"

After a minute, in a sepulchral tone, came the words, "Yes, when you weren't looking!"

Roy lay back on his pillows with a sigh.

A little disappointment mingled with his feelings which were somewhat mixed. After a pause, he said, "You *are* a good fellow! To think of doing that for me! What would you have done if I hadn't jumped in to save you?"

Then Dudley raised his head:

"I knew you wouldn't fail me," he said, triumphantly; "I knew I could trust you!"

Roy put out his thin little arm and drew Dudley's bonny face down by the side of his on the pillow.

"I don't think," he whispered, "that even I could have been plucky enough to do that—not in sight of that old mill wheel!"

Neither spoke for a few minutes; then Dudley said,

"I should have been your murderer if you had died. That has been the worst of it. But you did like saving a drowning fellow, didn't you?"

"Ye-es, but it wasn't quite real—at least it isn't as if you really had tumbled in by accident."

"Well but I only did what you said we must do. I made an opportunity."

And after this remark Roy had nothing more to say; but neither he nor Dudley ever enlightened any one as to the true cause of the accident.

When Roy had quite recovered, the two boys set out one afternoon to visit their greatest friend in the village. This was the old man every one called "old Principle." He lived by himself in a curious three-cornered house at the extreme end of the village, and kept a little general shop where everything but eatables could be obtained.

"I keep every article that man, woman, or child can want for their use, for their homes, their work or their play; but food and drink I will not cater for. It's against my principles to sell perishable goods, and I will not be the one to minister to the very lowest animal wants of my fellow creatures."

This was his favorite speech, from which it may be judged he was somewhat of a character.

He had several hobbies, and was a well-read man and superior to those around him; and perhaps this was the cause of his holding himself aloof from most of the villagers. They termed him "cranky and cracked," but his goods were always acceptable, and he was thoroughly successful in his business. When his shop was closed he would go out on the hills, and there spend his time studying geology and botany. He knew the name of every plant and insect, and the strata of the earth for many miles round; and it was out of doors that the boys first made his acquaintance.

They found him on this afternoon seated behind his counter mending an eight-day clock.

"Well, old Principle, how are you?" said Roy, climbing up to the counter and sitting comfortably on it with his legs dangling in mid air; "we haven't seen you for ages."

"Are you going out this evening?" enquired Dudley, as he proceeded to follow Roy's example.

"To be sure, when my work is done," responded the old man pushing up his spectacles and regarding the boys with kindly eyes; "these light evenings are my delight, as you know. If you sit still till I have finished this clock, I will show you a treasure I found yesterday."

"Can you mend everything?" asked Roy, curiously; "I never knew you understood about clocks."

"I've learned to mend most things," was the answer; "it isn't given to every one to make, and I'm one of the menders in the world not the makers. There's one thing I can't mend—and that is broken hearts."

There was silence: Roy broke it at last by saying with knitted brow, "I'd rather be a maker than a mender, but lots of people aren't either."

"Quite right," nodded the old man; "most folk are breakers."

"I wish I was as clever as you," said Dudley; "you mend umbrellas, and kettles, and plates, and windows, and gates, and all sorts. How did you learn?"

"Well, I ain't ashamed of owning that my father was just a travelling tinker, and when I was a little fellow I used to go round with him and see him do most things. It was from travelling through the country I learned to love it so.

And my father, he was a thoughtful man, and when I used to ask where the tin came from, and where the iron and where the lead, he took to learning of it up so that he could answer me; and then I came to find that most of our comforts come from underground, and so I fell to digging. Ah, youngsters, earth is a wonderful treasure house!"

The clock was done. Old Principle put it carefully by and then mounted on some wooden steps, and took down a tin saucepan. The boys knew the shelf well; as though apparently it was just a row of tinware for sale, many a pot and pan held treasures that geologists would have given a great deal to possess.

Now when old Principle held out a peculiar shaped stone with loving pride, Roy and Dudley pressed forward to look at it.

"I know, it's a Roman hammer," shouted out Dudley.

"It's a Saxon jug," suggested Roy.

"It's part of a jaw of a mammoth many thousands of years old, and there are two teeth in perfect preservation," old Principle said solemnly.

"Where did you find it?"

"Ah, you must come and see! In a cave that I have only just discovered, and which must originally have been by the side of a river. I'll take you there to-night if you can get permission to come."

Nothing delighted the boys more than an expedition with old Principle. They promised to be down at his shop punctually at half-past seven that evening, and then the conversation drifted into other channels.

"Old Principle, do you think we ought to make opportunities?" questioned Dudley, presently; "Roy thinks we ought, and I did make one the other day, but it didn't turn out well."

"Ay, Master Roy is always for making," said the old man with a smile; "he will try and cram his life with what will come fast enough naturally, if he only waits."

"But will it?" questioned Roy, flushing up with eagerness; "do you think it will? I'm longing to do something big and grand and good; I mayn't live to grow up you know, and I'm sure we're meant to do something when we're boys."

"We're trying to do good to all men as we have opportunity," said Dudley, gravely.

"Ay, stick to that, boys, and you'll succeed. There's none too small to be true philanthropists."

"What is a philanthropist?" asked Roy.

"A man who benefits his fellow creatures. 'Tis a good principle to keep in mind."

"But it's difficult for boys to do grown-up people good. They always do boys good."

"Now look here, Master Roy. I've lived and learned where you haven't, and I try and pass my principles on to you. That's how I do you good. You come to me and take what I give you and seeing you act out the advice I offers you does me good. You do me good too, every time you comes to see me; it's cheery to hear and see you."

"But that's very tame for us," said Roy, a little scornfully.

"Oh, well, if your own likes must come into the question, it's a different story! I didn't know it mattered about our feelings as long as the good is done! 'Tis a bad principle to try to please others only when it pleases ourselves."

Roy looked a little ashamed of himself. He said no more on the subject, and shortly after he and Dudley ran home to tea.

They were very disappointed when their aunt refused to let them go out again that evening.

"It is too damp a night for Jonathan to be wandering through wet grass and bog. You can go, David, if you like, but he must wait for another opportunity."

"I shan't go without Roy," said Dudley, sturdily.

"We'll come and make a cave in the attic," suggested Roy, trying to be cheerful.

And for the rest of that evening they were absorbed in making a great dust and racket amongst lumber boxes far away from their grandmother's hearing.

IV

AN AWKWARD VISIT

"And how do you know a river has been here?"

"By the soil and by the relics I have found. Look at this fossil. Do you see the outline of the fish? Fish don't live on dry ground."

"There might have been a fishman passing by who dropped one out of his cart."

Old Principle laughed at Dudley's sceptical notion, and went on shovelling out earth with great alacrity. It was Saturday afternoon: old Principle had shut up his shop and taken the boys up to the hills surrounding the little village, where in a ravine between two precipitous crags, in the midst of a green bower of ferns and moss, he was hard at work excavating an old cave that had been buried for many years out of sight.

Dudley and Roy were eagerly helping and chattering as only boys know how.

"This little ravine has been formed by a mountain stream rushing down," continued the old man, resting on his spade for a minute; "'tis a good principle, Master Dudley, to trust grown-up folks' knowledge better than your own."

"I wish," said Roy, reflectively, "that this cave was nearer home; it would be so lovely to come out whenever we wanted to, wouldn't it, Dudley? Perhaps some king has hidden away in it, or soldier when he was pursued by his enemies!"

"Hulloo," said Dudley, looking up the hill; "here is such a funny looking woman coming down with a donkey, her skirt is nearly up to her knees, and she has a man's boots on."

Old Principle paused in his work, and in a minute or two greeted the newcomer.

"Good-afternoon, Mrs. Cullen, how's your husband to-day?"

"Badly, very badly, but I's forced to leave he. I lock the door and put the key in me pocket, for I's bin up the hill yonner cuttin' peat sin seven o'clock this mornin'. He do get awfu' lonesome, he say, an' if me niece hadn't a married and gone to 'Merica, I should have kept she to tend him."

"Who is she?" asked Roy, as after a few more words the woman moved on.

"She lives at the bottom of the hill over there. Her husband has been ill of consumption these last two years, and she works to support them both. She's a hard-working woman, is Martha Cullen; she works in the fields harvesting just now; if I could feel I'd be welcome I would go to sit with her husband sometimes, but she's

Amy Le Feuvre

very queer, she won't let a neighbor come near him, I have tried more than once. It seems hard on him to be bedridden there day after day without a soul to speak to; or any one to give him a drink!"

Roy gazed thoughtfully after the retreating figure of the woman, and then turned his attention again to the cave.

When an hour later he and Dudley were walking home footsore, and rather dirty, but with little bundles of treasures from the cave in their grubby hands, he startled his cousin by saying—

"To-morrow we'll go and see Martha Cullen's husband. It's an opportunity for us."

"How shall we get in?" queried Dudley.

"Climb in at the window. She told old Principle she would be out all day at Farmer Stubbs. We'll go and do him good."

"How?"

"We'll wash his face, and make him a cup of tea, and sweep his room, and give him his medicine," responded Roy, readily; "that's what nurse does when she goes to visit any of Aunt Judy's sick people."

Dudley did not look as if he relished the prospect before him.

"That's girls' and women's work," he said; "boys needn't do that kind of thing."

Roy flushed up angrily.

"All right, if you don't want to come, stay at home. It is a week since we started to do good when the opportunity came, and we haven't done any good to any one. I'm not going to waste any more time."

Then after a pause he added, "Besides I think it will be rather fun breaking into a strange cottage; we may have to get down the chimney."

At this Dudley's face cleared.

"I'll come," he said; "we'll go directly after dinner."

"And we'll stow away a little of our pudding to take him—sick people always have puddings."

They had no difficulty in carrying out this plan. They always dined in the nursery, and if nurse wondered at the amount of pudding that her charges managed to consume that day, her old eyes were not sharp enough to detect the transfer from plates to pockets. She sent them out into the garden to play, and they soon were scampering out of the back gate and along the road toward the little cottage at the bottom of the hill.

It was a warm afternoon, and when they at length came near it they threw themselves down on the grass to rest.

"We mustn't frighten the old man," said Dudley, gazing at the thatched cottage with a critical eye. "I see the windows are tight shut in front, but there's one open at the side; we must creep up very quietly and get in before he sees us, and then we can explain who we are."

"And if the window won't do, we'll try the chimney, it looks a jolly big one."

Amy Le Feuvre

Then after a pause—

"I suppose he'll be glad to see us?"

"Of course he will. He must be dreadfully dull all alone."

A few minutes after, they were holding a whispered consultation outside a small pantry window through which Roy was going to squeeze himself.

"I'll go first. It will be a tight fit for you, Dudley, but I'll give you a good pull through, and you must hold your breath well in."

"It's a kind of housebreaking," Dudley said, ripples of fun passing over his face; "I don't mind visiting sick people if we go in at their windows like this!"

But Roy's little face was full of anxious gravity and purpose, and he checked Dudley's inclination to laugh at once.

He accomplished his part successfully, and then poor Dudley was hauled and pulled at till purple in the face, and breathless with exertion, he exclaimed, "I'm being squashed to a jelly; let go, I can't do it!"

"Just one more try—now then—there, we've done it!"

But Roy's exclamation of delight was drowned in an awful crash, as Dudley swept off some shelves a bowl of milk, two plates, and a cup of soup, and fell to the ground himself in the midst of it all.

Immediately a man's voice called out, "Who's there! Hi! Help! Thieves! Help!"

Roy darted into the kitchen, and confronted a tall, hollow-cheeked man who had scrambled out of his bed in the chimney corner, and stood trembling from head to foot clutching hold of the bed-post, and coughing violently.

He did not seem at all appeased at the sight of the boys, but shook his fist at them in a paroxysm of fright and rage.

"Go away, you young blackguards—a robbin' honest folk, and a darin' to show yer impudent faces, and disturbin' a dyin' man, knowin' as he's too bad to give yer the hidin' ye desarve!"

Roy was quite taken aback.

"You're quite mistaken—let us explain—we've come to see you and do you good. Don't you know who we are? We live at the Manor. Look—get back into bed again, you'll take cold. We've brought you some pudding."

Here a parcel of currant pudding was taken out of his jacket pocket and held out temptingly.

"A' don't believe a word! Ye've been in the pantry a smashin' the missus' things, and a eatin' and a drinkin' all ye can lay hands on—begone, I tell ye!"

"That was me," put in Dudley, edging up to the irate invalid; "you see the door was locked and we had to come in at the window, and I'm rather fat about the shoulders, and Roy jerked me through too quick and I fell amongst some plates. But we really haven't stolen anything, we aren't robbers!"

"Begone, ye rascals!" repeated the old man, and then such

a violent fit of coughing took possession of him that he sank back on his bed perfectly exhausted and helpless, waving them away and shaking his head at them when they tried to approach him.

Dudley looked doubtfully at Roy.

"I'm afraid we aren't doing him any good," he said, slowly. "He won't let us."

"No," was Roy's response, "we must go, I suppose. He is a foolish, stupid old man, or he would listen to us and let us explain."

Then advancing again to the sick man Roy said slowly and solemnly, "You'll be very sorry one day when you know how you've treated us, and we shall never, never try to see you again, or bring you pudding or comfort you, *never*! If you had let us, we should have washed your face and hands, and made you some gruel, and given you your medicine, and then sat down by your bed and talked nicely to you, but you won't let us do you good, so we shall leave you, and if you're lonely locked in here all day with no one to speak to, it's your own fault!"

Then holding his head up bravely, Roy marched out of the kitchen, and Dudley followed him with some misgivings as to his exit again by the pantry window. But Roy solved this difficulty.

"Look here, the key is in the back door; we will unlock it and get out properly. I'm sorry we've smashed those plates."

They walked home in the deepest dejection; as they went through the village there met them on the bridge the same man that had passed them when on the garden wall. He was much the worse for drink, and seemed inclined to be quarrelsome.

"Look 'ee here now, I'll just trouble 'ee to give me another sixpence, young gent, or I'll help myself, and no nonsense, for I'm the feller for fightin'!"

He stood barring their way, lurching from side to side, and brandishing a stick in his hand.

Neither of the boys were daunted. Dudley shouted out,

"Let us by at once, or we'll make you! You'd better look out how you cheek us!"

And Roy in a moment had his jacket off, and was rolling up his shirt sleeves.

"Come on, Dudley, we'll lick him into shape, if he dares to touch us!"

What might have befallen our two little heroes cannot be told, for at this critical juncture the rector came up, and in stern, commanding tones ordered the man on.

"That stamp of man is a pest in the place," he said; "he won't be influenced for good but hangs about the ale-houses and lives on the proceeds of his begging. If people only knew the harm they do in giving him money instead of a little honest work! Well, boys, run along home, it's a good thing I came up to stop a free fight. How do you think you two atoms could have got the better of a man like that? 'Discretion is the better part of valor' remember. Keep your fists for a good cause. And never entice a drunken man to fight. It is a degrading spectacle."

Amy Le Feuvre

Saying which Mr. Selby passed on, and Roy and Dudley walked home without saying a word to each other.

By the time they had finished their tea, they recovered their spirits, and were in the midst of an exciting game of cricket in a field adjoining the house with the old coachman and the stable-boy, when a summons came to them from the house to come in at once to their aunt.

"What's up, I wonder!" exclaimed Dudley, as he raced Roy up to the front door; "Aunt Judy never sends for us at dinner time."

They found their aunt in the library. She was in her dinner dress and the dinner gong was sounding in the hall, but her face was puzzled as she turned from a woman talking to her, to the boys.

"My nephews are little gentlemen; you must be mistaken," she was saying.

Roy and Dudley recognized the woman immediately. It was Mrs. Cullen, and their hearts sank.

"Come here, boys," Miss Bertram said; "I have been hearing a strange story from Mrs. Cullen, of two boys breaking into her house while she was away this afternoon, frightening her dying husband so much that the doctor fears he won't outlive the night, and breaking, and stealing things from her pantry. She insists upon it that it was you; her husband told her so, but I cannot believe it. You would have no object in behaving so wickedly."

Dudley's cheeks were crimson, and he hung his head in shame. Roy, as usual, was not daunted.

"It's all a great mistake, Aunt Judy, we never stole a thing; we went to see him and take him some pudding and do him good. We had to get in at the pantry window because the doors were all locked, and we did spill some milk and some soup, and broke a few plates. We couldn't make him understand we weren't robbers, so we came away again—and we're very sorry."

Mrs. Cullen turned furiously upon them, and her language was so abusive, that Miss Bertram sent the boys away, and brought the poor woman to reason by quiet, persuasive words.

"I will enquire into the matter. I cannot quite understand their motive; boys are thoughtless, and perhaps their intentions were good. I know they will be extremely sorry at the result of their visit. If you come with me to the housekeeper she will give you some good, strong soup for your husband. I will come and see him myself the first thing to-morrow morning."

It was not till after she had dined with her mother, that Miss Bertram sent for her little nephews again, and then she gave them a severer scolding than they had received from her for a long time. They crept up to bed that night feeling very woe-begone.

"I'm sure we'd better give up these opportunities," said Dudley, disconsolately, as they paused at an old staircase window on their way to their rooms; "you see this is the third one, and they all turn out badly. There was that tramp who must have got drunk with your sixpence, and then there was saving me, and that made you so awfully ill, and now here's this old fellow that perhaps we shall make die. It all goes wrong, somehow."

Amy Le Feuvre

Roy looked out of the window with knitted brow.

"I was thinking of that King—Bruce—who saw the spider try three times and then succeed. We must try again, that's all! I shan't give up yet. It is really a big opportunity I'm looking for!"

And Roy laid his head down on the pillow that night, steadfastly purposing to continue his role of benefiting the human race.

V

A LOST DONKEY

Fortunately for the boys, John Cullen got over his fright and took a turn for the better, but Miss Bertram began to exercise more control over their many spare hours. She took them out driving with her in the afternoon, or expeditions by foot; sometimes to some farmhouse to tea, sometimes to some neighboring squire who had young ones to entertain them. And Dudley in his happy, careless way soon put all thoughts of improved opportunities out of his head. He was ready enough to put into action any proposal of Roy's, but left alone he was perfectly content to enjoy himself in his own easy fashion; and Roy seemed to be willing to let the matter rest, as he never now alluded to it.

But one morning two or three weeks later, as the boys were returning from the Rectory with their satchels in their hands, they met an old man they knew in deep distress.

"What's the matter, Roger?" asked Roy; "why are you muttering away and shaking your head so?"

"Ay, young master, I be in a sorrowful plight. My donkey

has strayed away and I cannot find she nowheres. I've been up over the hills, and not a sign of she! And it's to-morrow that's market day, and how I'm to get my veggetubbles to town is more'n I can tell 'ee!"

"She can't be lost; when did you have her last?"

"'Twas yest'day mornin'. Ay, she be just a kickin' up her heels miles away and a laughin' at her poor old master. She be a terrible beast for strayin', and I just let her out on the green for a bit thinkin' to give her a pleasure, and that's how she treats me, the ungrateful creature! I heerd she were seen on the hills, but I'm a weary of trampin' up and down 'em."

"We'll go out on the hills and look for her this afternoon," said Roy, eagerly.

"If Aunt Judy will let us," added Dudley.

But Miss Bertram having gone out to lunch with some friends could not be asked, so the two boys set out after their early dinner with light hearts.

"It's doing old Roger good, and ourselves too," said Roy; "I'm longing to have a good outing, and we needn't be back very early, for granny isn't well enough to see us to-day, nurse said."

It was a delicious afternoon for a ramble; a soft breeze was blowing, and the sun was not unpleasantly strong. The boys did a good deal of looking for the missing donkey, but also managed to combine with that a few other things, such as bird-nesting, picking wild strawberries, and enjoying themselves as only boys can, when roaming about in the open air. At last rather late in the afternoon they spied in the distance a donkey, and delighted to think their quest was at an end, they hastened up to it.

Dudley had brought some carrots in his pocket, but the donkey was utterly indifferent to such a dainty; she waited till the boys were nearly up to her, and then with a kick up of her heels away she galloped, evidently enjoying the chase.

"Won't I give her a licking when I catch her," shouted Dudley, wrathfully, as after a long and tiring race, they stopped a minute to rest; "let us leave her and go home, Roy. I'm sure it's tea time, for I feel dreadfully hungry, and we're miles and miles away. I've never been so far before."

"Oh, we mustn't give up," Roy replied, with his usual determination; "we won't be beaten by an old donkey, and when we do catch her, we will both get on her back and ride her home. Come on, let us have another try!"

"We haven't got a halter, that's the worst of it."

But Dudley plucked up courage, and in another half hour they were successful; Roy seated on the donkey's back, and Dudley holding firmly to her tail.

"Now then—away with you—hip—hip—hurray!"

Away they tore, both donkey and boys in best of spirits now: but before long they were brought to a standstill. A man brandishing a huge stick sprang out in front of them.

"Now then, you rascals, what are you doing to my donkey? Get off it this instant!"

Amy Le Feuvre

"It isn't your donkey, it's old Roger's, and we're taking it home to him. Don't you cheek us! You're a rascal yourself!"

Dudley spoke angrily, but as he noticed the donkey stop instantly, and begin to sidle up toward the man an awful fear smote him, and Roy added quietly,

"You see you may be a thief or any one, for all we know, and it isn't likely we're going to let you have the chance of stealing old Roger's donkey. You go away and leave us alone. We're going home now—Gee-up. Come on, Dudley."

Not an inch would the donkey stir; and the man with a laugh, slipped a halter out of his pocket and in another minute Roy was rolling on the grass, and the donkey was being led off in the opposite direction.

"You may think yourselves lucky to escape the thrashing ye desarves!" shouted out the man; "ye've given me a nice chase after my beast for the last hour, and ye needn't add a pack of lies to your wicked pranks!"

The boys sat down on the grass to consider their position.

"Well, I call it beastly rot," grumbled Dudley, thoroughly cross; "if that's his donkey I don't believe old Roger's is on the hills at all. It must have been this one that somebody saw, and now I come to think of it Roger's has a black stripe down her back, and this one hadn't!"

"I'm so awfully tired," said Roy, disconsolately; "we've done no good as usual. I don't believe we ever shall do any one any good!"

When Roy's spirits sank it was a bad case, and for some minutes there was silence between them. Then feeling they must make the best of it they scrambled to their feet and plodded slowly on in the direction of home. A heavy mist was falling by this time, and dusk was setting in. Roy began to cough, and at last in despair Dudley cried out, "I do believe we're lost; I don't know where the path is, and I'm sure this isn't the way we came!"

"Well," said Roy, gasping as he spoke; "I'm afraid this old mist is getting into my chest, and I can't go very fast when my breath gets short. What shall we do? Can you shout— p'raps that man with the donkey might hear us."

Dudley shouted and shouted till he was hoarse, and then the little fellows trudged wearily on.

"You see," said Roy, bravely; "we must get somewhere if we go straight on."

"I believe," said Dudley, in doleful tones; "that you get right round the world and come back to where you started, if you only walk straight enough!"

This depressing view did not comfort his cousin.

"I've always thought it would be very exciting to be lost," Roy said with a sigh; "but it doesn't seem very nice, does it? And it is so cold. I wonder if we shall meet with any adventures, lost people generally do."

"If we could come into a gipsies' camp with a huge fire and a pot of stewed hares, it would be stunning! Or if we could find old Principle's cave, that would be better still!"

They were stumbling on, Roy gasping and panting for

Amy Le Feuvre

breath, and Dudley every minute or two giving a shout, when suddenly almost as if he had risen from the ground, a lad appeared in front of them.

"We're lost," shouted Dudley; "who are you? Can you tell us where Crockton village is?"

"Ay, can't I! You're only about four mile off!"

"Is it straight on?" questioned Roy, wistfully.

"No, you're goin' away from it."

The lad stood looking down at the two small boys and there was some pity in his tone.

"The little 'un is dead beat. Here—let me hoist you on my back, I'd as lief go to Crockton as anywhere else to-night, and I know every inch of these hills, I've been looking after cattle here since I were a babby! There now, ain't that better?"

Roy was too tired out to resist, though he made a faint protest, and Dudley seeing him comfortably settled on the broad shoulders of the lad, trotted along contentedly by his side.

"How did you find us? Did you hear us shouting?"

"I was trapping some moles close to yer, as ye came on."

"Where do you live? And what's your name?"

"I'm called Rob. I don't live nowheres now. Got chucked out last night!"

And Rob gave a short laugh as he spoke.

"Where from?"

"Well, you see there's a lot of us, and the old woman—she's my stepmother—she told me she wouldn't keep me no longer. My father—he died last year, and work is hard to get. I'll tramp into some town and try my luck there."

"Then where were you going to sleep to-night?"

"Sleep? Oh, bless yer—there's plenty o' room and accommodation in the open. And I haven't been about these parts for so long without knowing many a snug corner. I could show yer plenty a one. My pet one has been found out by some old chap lately. He goes into it and digs up quantities o' stones and then sits and hugs them, all as if they was gold! I laugh to see him sometimes!"

"Why that must be old Principle, and that's the cave he thinks so much of! He looks for bones."

Rob gave another of his hearty laughs.

"Well, if he has a taste that way, why don't he go to a churchyard, he'll dig to more success there."

"No, it's only animals' bones he likes, very, very old ones."

They tramped on, and then Roy asked if he could be put down, and Dudley given a lift instead. Rob good-naturedly assented, but some minutes were spent in altercation between the two boys before Dudley would consent to this arrangement.

Amy Le Feuvre

"You're as tired as I am," persisted Roy.

"Oh, no, I'm not—at least it's only my legs. You see I haven't a chest like you. I'll manage, it's always you that gets home ill, I never do."

"I can't help it," said Roy, in a shaky voice; "I know I shall never be good for anything, I don't think I'm much better than a girl, I suppose I ought to have been made one."

Roy was always in the depths of misery when he came to this climax, and Dudley hastened to reassure him.

"Rot! You're as good a walker as I any day. Yes, I'll have a ride on your back, Rob, if you like. I'm nearly done for, and Roy looks quite fresh again."

There was great commotion when the trio reached the Manor at last. Miss Bertram came out into the hall to greet them with an anxious face.

"Oh, you scamps! You'll turn my hair grey before long. Where have you been? Half the village has turned out to look for you! What mischief have you been up to?"

When the explanation was given Miss Bertram gave a little groan.

"If we are going to have these kind of expeditions, I really must insist upon your leaving off trying to do other people good. Old Roger told me he found his donkey quite early in the afternoon. Now come off to bed both of you. I believe nurse is already getting her poultice ready in anticipation of a bad night, Jonathan!"

"What is Rob going to do?" Roy asked, shortly after, when he was comfortably tucked up in bed, and was enjoying a hot basin of bread and milk. Miss Bertram had just come in to see how he was.

"Is that the lad that brought you back? He is having a good supper in the kitchen, and then will go home, I suppose."

"But he hasn't any home," said Roy, putting down his spoon and looking at his aunt with an anxious face; "he can't get work, so his mother turned him out of doors, and I want him to come and live with us, and when I grow up he shall be my servant!"

Miss Bertram laughed.

"My dear boy, not quite so fast. I shall not turn him out to-night, if he has no home to go to; but we cannot keep a lot of idle boys about the establishment."

Roy's brown eyes filled with tears. It was so rarely that he showed his feelings that his aunt began to wonder whether he was not too weak and exhausted from his walk to be talked to.

"Don't worry your little head over him," she said, kindly; "go to sleep, and I'll let you see him to-morrow morning."

"Have you ever been lost, Aunt Judy?"

Roy was struggling for self-command, and his voice was very quiet.

"No, I'm thankful to say I never have."

"I prayed to God," he went on solemnly; "that He would send some one to show us the way home, and Rob was the answer. And when he took me up on his shoulders and I knew he was taking me home, I thought of that picture over there!"

Roy pointed to a print of the Good Shepherd with the lost sheep across his shoulders, and Miss Bertram's face softened as she stooped and kissed her little nephew.

"Good-night dear. We will see what can be done."

She left the room and when nurse came bustling up to see if the bread and milk had disappeared she found her little charge gazing dreamily in front of him.

"Come, dearie, eat your supper. Don't you feel easier?"

"I was thinking," Roy said, slowly bringing back his gaze to the basin before him; "that if you're very strong you miss a lot of comfort; and however big and strong I grow up to be, I hope I shan't be too big and strong to be carried by Him!"

He pointed to the picture again, and good old nurse responded,

"If you outgrow the Lord, you'll outgrow heaven!"

VI

ROB

Roy was not allowed to go to the Rectory the next morning as it was rather damp, and nurse was carefully trying to ward off a bronchial attack, but he was permitted to see Rob, and the latter came in looking rather sheepish and as if he did not know what to do with his hands and his feet.

"What are you going to do, Rob?" asked Roy, eagerly, after their first greetings had been exchanged; "you aren't going home again?"

"I'd sooner be shot," was the short reply.

"I've been talking to Aunt Judy about you again this morning, and she says if you would like to help our old gardener in the garden and could get a character from some one, she'd try you. I don't quite know what she means about the character. I thought that belonged to you and not to any one else. She says she doesn't know what you're like, but I told her I'd find out. I say, take a chair, won't you. Now then, you don't mind my asking you a few questions, do you? Are you a thief?"

Rob took the chair that was offered him, squared his shoulders, and looked up with a pleasant smile at this blunt question.

"No, I ain't that."

"Have you ever killed anybody?"

"No."

"Are you a drunkard?"

"I hate the stuff!"

"Are you a fighter?"

"Well, no, not a reg'lar one. I can't say I've never knocked a feller down, or squared up with him a bit, but I don't fight till I'm driven to it."

"Are you a liar?"

"No."

Roy drew a sigh of relief, then continued: "Well, if you aren't any of those, I'm sure Aunt Judy will have you, I told her I knew you weren't wicked."

"But I ain't no scholar," said Rob, doubtfully; "I can't write nor read, and that's against a feller!"

"Oh, well, you won't have to read and write much in the garden. Old Hal can't read either, and he makes a cross for his name when he has to write it. But I suppose you can learn, can't you?"

Rob nodded.

"You see I played truant mostly when I was sent to school, and then I began to mind the cattle soon after I were eight year old, but if any body would start me, I believe I could pick it up."

"I'll teach you myself when I've nothing else to do," said Roy, grandly; "for I want you to be clever. I want you to come with me, when I'm grown up, to my big house. You shall be my head servant, and live with me always. Would you like that?"

Rob grinned, and seemed to think it a great joke.

Roy continued: "Of course I shall want you more when Dudley goes away. He has got a stepfather, so when he grows up he will go out to India, I expect, to live with him, but we don't talk of it, and we pretend we're never going to leave each other. Did you find Dudley very much heavier to carry than me?"

"Well, yes, he were a bit heavier."

"I'm afraid I shall never catch him up, he is nearly a head taller, and he seems to grow quicker every month. I grow so slowly. I think it is because I lie in bed so much more than he does, I'm always having to go to bed in the daytime when I'm ill, and that must keep you from growing, don't you think so?"

The conversation was here interrupted by Miss Bertram's entrance. She had a long talk with Rob, and in the end took him for a month on trial, as she had known his father.

The boys were delighted, but Roy still persisted in regarding him as his special protege, and more than once this had occasioned a heated argument between the two cousins.

"He doesn't belong to you. You order him about as if he were your servant," said Dudley, impatiently, one afternoon after Roy had sent Rob on more than one errand to the house for him.

"Well, so he will be one day," returned Roy, flushing up.

They were seated again in their favorite corner on the wall, some ripe plums having just been handed up to them by the obliging Rob, and Dudley having put an extra big one in his mouth was speechless for a moment.

"I suppose you'll get so fond of Rob, that you won't want me any longer," he said, after some consideration.

"Rob is my servant, but you're a friend and relation," asserted Roy.

"He is an opportunity, and a pretty big one, isn't he?"

"Why, yes; I never thought of that! How splendid!"

Roy's large eyes were shining, and he gazed with tender pride at Rob who was now sweeping the lawn.

"We have done him good already, haven't we?" pursued Dudley, reflectively; "only he started by doing us good. I tell you what we might do for him. Teach him to read."

Roy looked very doubtful.

"It is so difficult, and he seems so stupid. I did try the other day, for he asked me to; but I never thought any body *could* be so stupid! I told him we would have to give it up, for it made me lose my temper so. I thought perhaps he could go to old Principle. You see he is too big for school, but old Principle is always saying he likes to teach people things."

"Well, that is awfully funny," said Dudley, pointing down to the pine woods opposite them. "Talk of him and there he is! Isn't that him walking along over there? Look—now he's stooping down to look at something. I'm sure it's old Principle; we'll call him!"

Two shrill boyish voices rang out, "Old Principle! Hi! We want you! Old Principle!"

Soon after old Principle was standing beneath the wall, having obeyed the summons.

He stood looking up at them with his straw hat pushed to the back of his head, and his keen, piercing eyes twinkling kindly under his thick, shaggy eyebrows.

"Well, laddies, you're above me now. 'Tisn't often you can look down at old Principle from such a superior height."

"We want to ask you if we may send Rob down to you for you to teach him to read," said Roy, eagerly.

"And why have not two idle boys more time than a busy shopkeeper to do such a thing?" demanded the old man.

"Oh, well, you see," explained Roy, confusedly; "grown-up people know how to teach, and boys don't. Besides, we aren't idle, we work hard at lessons all the morning, and we have half an hour's prep after tea."

Old Principle shook his head.

"And you're the lad for making people better, and doing good to all. 'Tis a bad principle, my boy, to wait for great opportunities, and let the small ones go!"

"Do you think we ought to teach him?" questioned Dudley.

"If he wants to learn, and you have the time, you will be letting the opportunity slip, that's all. And moreover old Principle isn't going to be the one to help you do it."

The old man turned his back upon them and walked into the pine wood again, leaving the two boys gazing after him with perturbed faces.

"He's rather cross this afternoon," observed Dudley.

"I s'pose he thinks it's for our good. Shall we try again? Could you teach him one day, and me the next? That wouldn't be quite so tiring."

Rob was called upon and consulted, and it was finally arranged that every afternoon from two to three he should have a reading lesson on the top of the garden wall.

"We shan't feel sleepy here, and it's the time everybody else is taking a nap," said Roy, trying to take a cheerful view of it. "I'm going to try and be very patient and not be cross once, for you're our opportunity, or one of them, isn't he, Dudley?"

Dudley nodded. "The biggest we've had yet," he said.

Rob grinned and went away delighted. He was a steady, honest lad, devoted to both boys; but especially to Roy, who, without Dudley's constant remonstrance, would have tyrannized over him to his heart's content. Miss Bertram left them alone; she exercised a certain supervision over Rob's work, but never objected to his joining her little nephews' amusements.

"They will not learn any harm from him," she told her mother; "and he may teach them many things that are good."

So it came to pass that reading lessons took place regularly every day on the top of the wall, and Rob's eagerness to master all hard words, and his humble diffidence, when his little teachers waxed wrath with him, was touching to witness. Sometimes conversation would bear a large part in the lessons, especially when Roy was the teacher. And Dudley would always insist on having a break for refreshments.

"You will be able to write letters for me, Rob, when I grow up," said Roy, one afternoon, pausing in the lesson. "I don't like writing letters, and I'm thinking of travelling round the world and discovering countries, so I shall have to write home sometimes. You will come with me, won't you?"

"For certain I will," was the emphatic reply.

"I've been thinking," pursued Roy, thoughtfully, as he let his gaze wander from the book between them to the top of the dark pines swaying gently in the summer breeze; "that I may be quite strong enough when I grow up to be a discoverer. You see I can't be a soldier or sailor, but I haven't anything the matter with me but a weak chest, and doctors say sea voyages and travelling do weak chests good sometimes. Do you think I'm a very poor body to look at, Rob? That's what some of the villagers say I am, but my head and legs and arms are all right. I'm not a cripple or a hunchback, or blind, or deaf, or dumb, so I must be very glad of that. What do you think?"

"You're just as straight and plucky as Master Dudley, and you'll grow up a big, strong man, I dare say," said Hob, sympathetically.

"Old Principle says you may be a maker, a mender, or a breaker in your life. I want to be a maker. And I should like to find a country and make it into a nice big town. I want to do something big. I ask God every day to let me find something to do."

"Do you believe in—in God?" asked Rob, rather sheepishly.

"Of course I do; what do you mean? Don't you?"

"I don't know. I don't know much about Him, only you often talk as if you're—well quite friends with Him, and I've wondered at it."

Roy brought down his gaze from the hilltops to his companion's face with grave interest.

"I've known God since I was a baby," he said. "I don't remember when I didn't know Him. Nurse used to talk to me when I was very small, and when my father was dying he called me to him, and said,—'Fitz Roy! Serve God first, then your Queen, and then your fellow men!' I've always remembered it, only you know we don't talk about these things, and I've only told Dudley. I'm trying to serve

God—you don't want to be very strong to do that; but I'm longing to serve the Queen, and when Mr. Selby talked to us of opportunities for doing good to all men I've been longing to find them ever since. Don't you know much about God, Rob?"

Rob shook his head. "I used to larn He made the world and me, and I know He'll punish the wicked, but I've never tried to serve Him, and—and I don't think as how I care about it."

"P'raps you don't know about Jesus Christ?" asked Roy, solemnly.

"Well, yes, I used to larn about Him when I was a kid at the Sunday-school. I know He came into the world to save people, but I never rightly understood why, nor what difference it makes."

"I'll be able to tell you that. If He hadn't died, I suppose I shouldn't have cared about serving God because it would have been no use—nothing would have been any use, for we should all have had to go to hell when we died, to punish us for our sins. We could never have got to heaven at all."

"If we had been very good I reckon we could," put in Rob, knitting his brows with this aspect of the subject.

"But you see the Bible says we can't be good, not one of us—the devil won't let us."

"But there are good people in the world."

"You interrupt so," said Roy, a little impatiently. "I was going to tell you. Jesus died to let God be able to forgive us and take us to heaven. It's rather difficult to explain, but God punished Him *instead* of us, do you see? So now we can all go to heaven, and the reason we try to be good is to please Jesus because He has loved us, and the reason we are able to be good is because Jesus helps us to be, and He can fight the devil better than we can. There, I think I've told you it right. Now shall we go on with the reading?"

Rob said no more till after the lesson was over, then he said slowly, "It's rather strange, that what you were a tellin' me, but I don't see it quite. P'raps another day you'll tell me again."

"If you make haste and read, I'll give you a Bible, and then you'll be able to read about it yourself. Of course you ought to be serving God just as much as anybody else, and you'd better begin at once!"

Saying which Roy scrambled down from his high perch and raced across the garden to the stables where he had settled to meet Dudley; whilst Rob descended more slowly, muttering to himself, "'Tis a good thing not to be afraid of God like Master Roy, but I doubt if I should ever get to serve Him!"

VII

A WALNUT STOKY

"I say, Dudley, do come out for a ride! Aunt Judy is with granny, and she says the house must be quiet, and I hate being in a quiet house. Come on! What are you doing?"

Roy finished his sentence by springing on Dudley's back, and as he was in a crouching attitude in a corner of the old nursery, he brought him flat to the ground by his unexpected attack. For a minute or two both boys rolled on the ground in each other's clutches, and feet and hands were having a busy time of it. Then Dudley sprang to his feet.

"I like you coming in to tell me to be quiet, and then beginning a fight at once! Do shut up! You've quite spoilt my last letter!"

"Well, what are you doing?"

"I'm carving my name in the corner here, just below my father's."

Roy looked with curiosity at Dudley's handiwork.

Amy Le Feuvre

"Yes, your M is very crooked; but I wouldn't choose to write my name on the wainscoting. It's too low down. I like to be at the top of everything. Now if you carved it on the ceiling that would be something like!"

"You're always wanting to do impossibilities!"

"I should like to have a try at them," rejoined Roy, quickly. "I hate everything that is easy. Now come on, do! and we'll have a good gallop over the down!"

Half an hour later and the boys were tearing through the village on their ponies, and were soon out on an open expanse of heather and grass.

Roy was in the midst of an eloquent harangue on all he was going to do when he was grown up, when Dudley suddenly came to a standstill.

"Something is the matter with Hazel. I believe she's going lame. Oh, I see, one of her shoes is loose! Now what are we to do!"

He sprang off his pony as he spoke, and looked perplexed at this calamity.

"Lead her on gently," was Roy's ready advice. "We aren't far off from C—, and I know there's a blacksmith there."

Dudley grumbled a little at having his ride spoiled in this fashion; but it was not long before they reached the neighboring village, and the smith's forge was soon found.

Then, whilst Hazel was being attended to, Roy suggested that they should go and see an old lady, a great friend of their aunt's, who lived just outside the village.

"She might ask us to tea," suggested Roy, "and she has awfully nice cake always going. I'll leave my pony here, and we'll call again for them on our way back."

"I don't like paying visits," objected Dudley, a little crossly.

"But Mrs. Ford isn't half bad to talk to, she's full of stories."

And by dint of these two baits, "cake" and "stories," Dudley's shyness was overcome, and the two boys were soon walking up a sunny little garden and knocking at the rose-covered door of "Clematis Cottage."

It was a tiny house, but spotlessly clean and tidy, and the long, low, dainty drawing-room into which they were shown had a sense of rest and repose which insensibly affected even the boys' restless spirits.

"A nice room to be ill in," was Roy's comment; "there would be such a lot of jolly pictures and things to look at on the walls when you were in bed."

"I should like to sit here on Sunday," said Dudley. "I am sure I could be still for quite half an hour!"

The door opened and a little old lady in widow's cap and gown came forward. She was a fragile, delicate-looking little woman, with a very bright face and smile, and she beamed upon the boys delightedly.

"My dear boys, this is quite a treat! I don't often get a visit from young gentlemen. How is your grandmother? Have you brought me any message from your aunt?"

"Granny is not very well to-day," replied Roy, frankly, "and Aunt Judy didn't know we were coming here. We have been riding, and Dudley's pony has had to be shod, so we've left him at the blacksmith's and come on here. You see we thought it would pass the time."

"And so it will, and you shall have a nice cup of tea before you go back. Why, what big boys you are growing! Which is the elder? I always forget."

"I am," said Roy, a little shamefacedly; "but of course most people think Dudley is, because he is the biggest."

"It's only two months and five days, though, between us," put in Dudley, eagerly, knowing what a sore point his size was to Roy; "and you see, Mrs. Ford, Roy's brain is much bigger than mine—Mr. Selby says it is, so that makes us quits!"

"And I wonder which has the biggest soul?" said Mrs. Ford, quaintly.

The boys stared at her.

"Shall I tell you a little story while we are waiting for tea?" she asked, sitting down in her easy chair by the open window, and looking first at the boys with loving interest, and then away to the sweet country outside her garden.

Roy gave Dudley a delighted nudge with his elbow.

"Yes, please; we love a good rattling story; and make plenty of adventures in it, won't you?"

But Mrs. Ford shook her head with a little smile.

"I can't tell you of fights with red Indians, and ship-wrecks, and lion hunts, and all such things as that; but you must take my story as it is, and think over it in your quiet moments.

"There was once an old garden. Flowers and fruit of every description grew in it, and when no human creature was about the air was full of flower laughter and fruit conversation. One day in autumn some saucy sparrows were teasing a young walnut-tree that stood between an apple and a pear-tree, opposite a wall which was covered with beautiful golden plums.

"'What are you here for?' they said, pecking at the round green balls that hung on the tree, and then wiping their beaks in disgust on the grass underneath. 'Ugh! you're sour and bitter and nasty enough to poison a person! You're a disgrace to your master. The red and yellow apples next door to you are delicious this warm day, and the pears make one's mouth fairly water, while as to the plums over there—well, every one is fighting for them, from the slugs and snails to every bird in the country, and the boys and girls and men and women—all of us have to be kept off by those horrible nets which the old gardener is continually spreading!'"

"'I'm sure,' whispered the young walnuts, humbly, 'we don't mean any harm. We don't quite know why we are here ourselves. We have been hoping to see our green skins get red and yellow, and soft and ripe, like every-thing else round us, but they seem to get harder and uglier as time goes by. They feel very heavy, and our stems ache with holding them up; do you think it just possible there may be something inside?'"

"'Inside!' laughed the sparrows; 'who ever heard of the

inside being better than the outside? You're stuffed with conceit, but nothing else.'"

"And away they flew, for they were not a year old themselves, and knew nothing about autumn nuts and berries.

"The walnuts sighed and appealed to an old crow flying by.

"'Do you think we have been planted in this beautiful garden by mistake?' they said. 'We have been waiting a long time to give pleasure and to do good to those around us. The bees give us a wide berth—they say they can get no honey from us; we have no sweet scent to please the passer-by, no lovely blossoms to delight their eyes. The apples have had blossoms and fruit, and all the other trees the same, yet here we hang and grow, and the days go by and we're only laughed at for our ugliness and want of sweetness.'"

"'Wait a little longer,' said the old crow; 'wait, and take pains to grow!'"

"And the walnuts waited, and the sun kissed their hard skins, and the rain refreshed them when dry and thirsty; and still the sparrows mocked them, and the apple and pear-tree talked to each other over their heads, for they too looked upon them as a failure. One day the biggest walnut broke from his stem and dropped in the long grass. No one heeded his fall except his brothers; the gardener came by and gathered the apples and pears, but did not look at the walnut-tree; and when he kicked the fallen walnut with his feet he took no more notice of it than if it had been a pebble.

"'Is that our fate?' sighed the walnuts. 'Now we know we

are no good. What is the use of trying to grow? What is the good of living at all when we're so ugly and useless, and the end of us is to lie and rot in the grass and be kicked by every one who passes?'"

"And they wept bitter tears of disappointment and mortification; and one by one they dropped from the tree and lay unheeded, uncared for on the ground below."

"Then one morning came up the old crow."

"'Why did you tell us to wait?' cried one walnut in petulant tones. 'We're rotting, dying here, and this is the end of us.'"

"'Wait a little longer,' said the crow again; 'it is when we are very low that we are lifted very high. When we come to an end a new beginning is coming.'"

"The walnuts sighed as he flew away; yet the biggest one turned with a spark of hope to his brothers."

"I do believe we have been made for something. My skin is rotting and dying, but in spite of it all I feel as if I have something inside that is still alive. Let us wait and be patient a little longer."

"And then at last one day, when the apple and pear-tree were fruitless and leafless, when the flowers and butterflies and bees had all disappeared, down the garden came the master himself and the gardener."

"He stopped when he came to the walnut-tree, and stooping down in the long grass he gently raised one of the fallen nuts."

Amy Le Feuvre

"'You must gather these in,' he said to his gardener; 'we have a good many for the first year.'"

"'Yes,' said the gardener, 'they are ready now. I've let them lie till you saw them.'"

"And the walnuts whispered to themselves in surprised delight that it was not neglect and indifference had left them there, but that the gardener had watched each one fall, and knew where to find them when their time came at last.

"And when their green husks were removed, and their brown shells cracked at the master's table, they discovered that the most valuable part of them was what could not be seen by outsiders, and could only be brought to light by the master's hand."

"That's a kind of parable," said Roy when Mrs. Ford ceased speaking.

"Yes," she said, smiling; "most people are like the sparrows: they think it is only the outside you should go by. Now, when I see a person for the first time I always wonder what their soul is like. If that is beautiful it doesn't matter about their body. And a little body may contain a very big soul."

"Can we make our souls big?" asked Roy, with an anxious face.

"They should be growing, my boy, day by day. Put them into the Gardener's keeping and He will make them grow. It isn't the handsome and the strong who do all the good in the world; very often it is just the other way."

"Then there is hope I may do something," said Roy, brightening up; "I like that story about the walnuts, don't you, Dudley?"

"Yes, I'll think of it when I crack them next," said Dudley.

Tea was now brought in, and the boys did it full justice, and shortly after they were on their homeward way.

"She's a jolly old thing," remarked Dudley, presently, "and her cake was awfully good. I'm glad we went to see her."

Roy was unusually silent. Dudley continued—

"I expect you've got the biggest soul of us too, Roy; nurse is always saying your soul is too big for your body."

"I wish I had no body sometimes," said Roy, with a sigh; "it gets so tired and stupid."

"Well, we won't talk about souls and bodies any more," Dudley said, quickly, "they aren't interesting. I say, do you think we could teach Rob cricket?"

Rob was a topic which always interested Roy. He brightened up at once.

"We'll teach him everything," he said, eagerly. "I want him to be able to read and write and play, and do everything that we do, and more besides, for I shall have him for my friend as well as a servant when I grow up."

"A funny kind of chap for a friend," said Dudley, a little crossly; "he's twice as old as you are, to begin with, and he's an awfully stupid, thick-headed fellow."

"Don't you like Rob?"

Roy's tone was an astonished one.

"Oh, I like him well enough, but I'm getting rather sick of hearing you crack him up so."

Roy changed the subject. He wondered sometimes why Dudley seemed to lose his temper so over Rob; it never entered his head that Dudley might regard him as a possible rival; that Rob, the country lad, might spoil the covenant of friendship between them.

VIII

THE BERTRAMS' LEAP

It was Roy's birthday, and he was standing at his bedroom window before breakfast looking out into the old garden below, his busy brain full of thought and conjecture. His birthday was a very important day to him, and for some years now there had been a settled programme for the day. His guardian, an old Indian officer living in the neighborhood, and formerly a very old friend of his father's, always came over to see him and stayed to lunch, the two boys joining their elders at that meal. Directly after, they would drive or ride over to Norrington Court which was Roy's future home, and stay there for the rest of the day.

The boy's heart was full of the future as usual, and when Dudley burst into his room with a radiant face to offer his good wishes, he turned to meet him gravely.

But Dudley was too occupied in tugging in a small basket to notice it.

"This is my present, old chap. Just open it and see if you don't like it."

Roy's little face became illumined with smiles a moment after, when he saw two beautiful little white mice amongst the straw looking up at him with calm curiosity out of their bright beady eyes.

"They're tame," said Dudley, delightedly; "old Principle has had them, taming them for over a month. Their names are Nibble and Dibble. Look! This is Dibble with the little black spot on his nose. You never guessed, did you? I've been down to see them lots of times and they'll eat food out of my hand. You just see!"

Roy was too excited over his mice to eat much breakfast, and when Rob came up to him immediately afterward with a new cricket ball, bought out of his small wages, he declared he was the "luckiest fellow in the world."

Miss Bertram presented him with a handsome writing case, and every one of the servants had some trifle to offer him. At ten o'clock he went to his grandmother's room.

This was also part of the programme.

Mrs. Bertram received him very impressively, as was her wont.

"Sit down, Fitz Roy; you are getting a big boy; have you been measured this morning?"

"Yes, granny, and I really have grown an inch and a half since last year. That isn't very bad, is it?"

"Your father was very much taller at your age. I cannot understand it."

Roy began to feel rather depressed. "General Newton will

be here soon, I suppose," continued Mrs. Bertram, precisely, "and I wish you to convey him a message from me. Give him my very kind regards, and ask him to excuse me from coming down to see him this morning. I have had a very bad night, and am not feeling fit for any extra fatigue. I hope he will find you improved in manners and appearance. I could wish you talked and laughed less and thought more. You must endeavor to realize your responsibilities when you visit Norrington Court this afternoon. It is a very large and important property for a little boy like you to be heir to, and I hope you will fill the position worthily when you come of age. Your uncle was the most respected and honored man in the county, and if your dear father had lived to come back from Canada, he would have walked in your uncle's steps."

"And who will walk in mine when I'm dead, granny?"

"My dear, you must learn not to interrupt grown-up people when they are speaking."

"I'm very sorry, but do tell me if I died before I grew up, would Dudley have my house?"

"Yes, by the terms of the will he would, as his father came next in age to yours."

"That is what Aunt Judy means, when she calls me Jonathan and says when I brag, that I must remember my namesake never came to the throne at all. I like to think that Dudley may have it, he would make a grander master than me, wouldn't he?"

Mrs. Bertram gave a little sigh. Roy's delicacy was a sore point with her, and she could never get reconciled to his small stature.

"Well," said Roy, after a pause; "I'll do my very best, granny, to grow up a big strong man. I take my tonics now whenever nurse gives them to me, and I never pour them out of the window as I used to do. And I'm hoping to do something great before I die, and I'm trying to grow up a good man. Do you think that will do?" he added, a little anxiously, as he fancied his grandmother's gaze rested on him with some dissatisfaction.

She did not reply, only drew out her purse from her pocket, and Roy knew this was a signal for his dismissal.

"Now," said Mrs. Bertram, "this is the sovereign that I usually give you. I hope you will spend it wisely. Tell me when it is gone what you have done with it. I hope you will spend a happy day. Give me a kiss and leave me. Oh, if only you were more like your handsome father!"

Roy took his gift, thanked her for it, and giving his grandmother a kiss, left the room very quietly.

Outside the door he paused on the door-mat, and drew his jacket across his eyes with a strangled sob.

"It's a pity God won't make me strong, but I don't seem to be able to do it myself."

And then with a shout for Dudley, a minute after he was tearing round the house, showing his pet mice to all, and chattering away as if he had not a care upon him.

General Newton arrived soon after and took a more cheering view of his ward's appearance than had his grandmother.

"You'll grow into a splendid fellow yet," he said, patting him on the shoulder, "and you'll out-top your cousin. Have you been in many scrapes lately?"

"They're good boys on the whole," replied Miss Bertram, smiling; "except when they try to be philanthropists, and then they come to grief."

"Oh, that's the last idea, is it? When I was here before they were going to be travelling peddlers. Have you made a choice of any profession yet, either of you?"

"Yes, I'm going to be a traveller and discoverer," said Roy, with decision.

"Oh, indeed! Then you've still the love for exploration. How is your friend old Principle? Is he still unearthing wonders and keeping them in his kettles?"

"He is busy in a cave now," said Dudley, eagerly; "would you like to come and see it one day?"

"No, thank you. And are you lads still devoted friends?"

"David and Jonathan, still," said Miss Bertram; and the old general laughed heartily.

Before he left, he also gave Roy a sovereign, which made the little fellow confide to Dudley,

"I've put granny's in my right hand pocket, and the general's in my left, they won't mix together well, because hers is such a solemn one, and his is so jolly!"

It was a happy little party that set off for Norrington Court. The boys were on their ponies, and Miss Bertram in her pony trap, with Rob sitting behind, proud in the consciousness of a new suit of clothes, and delighted at being included in the number.

Up a long stately avenue of elms and beeches, with bracken and ferns covering mossy glades in the distance, and then Roy and Dudley flung themselves off their ponies before an old stone house with ivy-covered walls and turrets. Everything had been brightened up for their visit. The flowers on the terraces were one mass of sweet perfume and color, the drives weeded and rolled, and the velvet turf in only such a condition as centuries of care can make it. The old housekeeper opened the door in her very best black silk, and two or three more faithful retainers stood in the background.

Roy spoke to them all with boyish frankness and grace, and then eagerly demanded if tea might be on the terrace. Miss Bertram agreed and while she went indoors for a chat with the housekeeper, the boys tore round the place dragging Rob after them. The stables of course were visited, and an old groom who had known the boys' fathers when boys, welcomed them with great warmth.

"Ye must grow quicker, Master Fitz Roy. We want to see you here among us. I'm looking to see all these stalls occupied by hunters and sich like again. 'Tis mournful work to live year in and year out with only two bosses for company!"

"Tell us about the old times, Ben, do!"

Ben sat down and spread his hands out on his knees reflectively.

"All the young gentlemen were born riders," he said,

slowly; "I mind how Master Randolph would tear up the avenue after a long ride. 'There, Ben' he'd say to me, chucking me the rein, and jumpin' off as light as a feather, 'we've worked our spirits h'off—Ruby and me!' When the old squire were alive, he'd have all three young gentlemen up, and then he'd mount them and bring them down to Ruddocks stream, and see them jump it. He used to say, 'No grandson of mine is worth calling a Bertram if he can't take that leap before he is twelve year old!' They all did it before they was ten, and he used to stand chuckling and rubbing his hands as he saw them do it."

"Is that the stream at the bottom of the back meadow?" asked Dudley, eagerly; "the one with the hedge in front?"

"Ay, to be sure!"

"But we have never jumped it," exclaimed Roy. "And I think we ought to for we're his great-grandsons."

"We shan't be twelve for a long time yet," said Dudley, "but we really ought to try."

"Well, we'll do it this evening after tea; and you shall come and see us do it, Ben."

Ben grinned from ear to ear.

"You'll go over it like a bird, if so be as your pony is accustomed to sich things!"

"We haven't taken very high jumps," admitted Dudley, candidly.

"Oh, we shall do it," said Roy, with a little toss of his head; "we'll *make* them go over!"

Amy Le Feuvre

And then they turned to other subjects.

"What do you think of my house, Rob?" asked Roy, later on as he was escorting his humble friend through the empty rooms and corridors upstairs.

"It'll take a powerful number of people to fill it," said Rob, with awe.

"I shall have a lot of friends to stay with me, of course, and then I shall marry; men always do that, don't they?"

"I b'lieve they mostly does," was the grave reply.

"And won't you like to come and live with me here?"

"That I should."

"Well," said Dudley, from a few paces behind; "if you're going to travel, you won't use your house much, Roy. If Rob is going to be your follower, I'll come and live here when you're abroad, and when you come home, I'll go away."

"No you won't, you know we shall want you too."

And seeing the frown on Dudley's face, Roy turned back and linked his arm in his. "Look here," he added, "Rob shall be your follower as well as mine, and we will all go out to look for a new country together, and when we've found it, we will come back and have a jolly time in this old house."

"I shall have to work for my living," Dudley replied, gruffly.

"Yes. I was thinking," and the earnest look came into Roy's eyes as he spoke; "I was thinking this morning, I mustn't just live as I like to live when I grow up. There will be an awful lot to be done. Old Principle was telling me the other day that the reason some people are overworked is because other people don't work enough, and an idle man puts his burden of work on other people's backs."

"We don't want old Principle's sermons here," exclaimed Dudley, having recovered his good humor. "Aren't you awfully hungry? I'm sure tea must be ready."

They went to the terrace where a most elaborate repast was set out, which they thoroughly enjoyed. After it was over all the servants came up to drink Roy's health; the old butler Pike made a little speech, and Roy responded; his words lingering in the memories of those who heard him for long afterward.

Miss Bertram, as she looked at his upright, slender little figure, and noted the intense emphasis with which he spoke, felt a pang go through her, as she wondered if his frail young life would be cut short before he reached manhood.

"I'm awfully much obliged to you all for your good wishes. I'm determined when I grow up and come to live with you that I'll do all the good I can to everybody. I hope I'm getting stronger, and I think I may be able to do as much as other people. But whatever I am, I promise you I'll do my very best for the property!"

Then three cheers were given for the little master; and after the ceremony was over, Miss Bertram told her little nephews to amuse themselves quietly for another half

Amy Le Feuvre

hour before they returned home.

Their plans were already arranged, and they went straight to the stables for their ponies to try the leap the old groom had mentioned to them.

He had already saddled them, and a few minutes after, they came through the small paddock in front of the spot.

It was rather an awkward hedge, though not a very high one with a broad stream of running water the other side.

Old Ben began to get a little nervous as he saw the boys eyeing the leap rather doubtfully.

"Has the hedge grown since our fathers were little boys?" asked Dudley.

"A wee bit, perhaps, though we do keep it cut pretty much to the same level. It's a deal thicker than it used to be, but don't you try it if you hain't sure of your ponies. It 'ud be a awful thing if you hurt yourself and couldn't do it!"

"If we try it at all, we shall do it," said Roy, spiritedly, and then he and Dudley rode back to put their steeds to a gallop.

Old Ben watched them breathlessly. Dudley seemed to be hesitating.

"I say, old fellow, don't let us do it to-night."

Roy's look was one of astonishment mingled with a little contempt.

"Not do it! Are you afraid?"

Dudley's color rose. "I'm not afraid of our courage," he said, boldly, "but of our ponies: they have never been accustomed to it."

"Then they can learn to-night. Now then, there's plenty of room for us both abreast. One—two—three—off! Hurrah for the Bertrams!"

The ponies were fresh, the hedge was cleared; but as old Ben was in the act of waving his cap aloft to give a cheer —there was a crash—a sharp cry—and a sickening thud the other side of the hedge. And when the old groom with beating heart and trembling limbs, reached the farther bank, Roy and his horse were prostrate on the ground. Dudley had cleared it safely, and now having flung himself from his horse was leaning over Roy in agony of terror.

"He's dead, Ben—he's dead—his pony rolled over him— oh, fetch a doctor, quick!"

Ben took the unconscious little figure in his arms, with a heavy groan; and Dudley tore on to the house almost frantic with fright.

Every one was in confusion at once, but it was Rob who tore off for the doctor, and brought him in an incredibly short time, considering that he lived three miles away.

To Dudley, listening outside the bedroom door, it seemed years before the doctor came out, and when he did, he was too overcome to speak to him. But seeing the white unnerved face of the boy, Doctor Grant put his hand kindly on his shoulder.

"Cheer up, my boy, it might have been worse—he is only

stunned, and leg broken. I hope he will pull round again."

And then Dudley burst into a passionate fit of tears, with relief at the doctor's words.

IX

MAKING HIS WILL

It was long before the cousins met; Roy's delicate constitution had received such a shock that his condition for
some time was a cause of grave anxiety. His leg did not
heal, and then the terrible word was whispered through
the house "amputation"!

It was a lovely evening in September when after a long
talk with the doctor in the library Miss Bertram came out,
her usually determined face quivering with emotion.

"I will tell him to-night, Doctor Grant, and we shall be
ready for you to-morrow afternoon at three."

She went upstairs, and Dudley with scared eyes having
heard her speech now crept out of the house after the
doctor.

"Look here, Doctor Grant," he said, confronting him with
an almost defiant air: "you're not going to make Roy a
cripple!"

"I'm going to save his life, if I can," said the doctor, half
sadly, as he looked down upon the sturdy boy in front

Amy Le Feuvre

of him.

"He won't live with only one leg, I know he won't, it will be too much of a disgrace to him; he'll die of grief, I know he will! Oh, Doctor Grant, you might have pity on him, it isn't fair!"

"Would you rather see him die in lingering pain?" enquired the doctor, gravely.

"Oh, I think it so awful! Why should he be the one to be smashed up. Look at me! I know everybody thinks it a pity it wasn't me. It would have made us so much more equal. Why should I be so strong, and he so weak! I tell you what! I've heard a story about joining on other men's legs. Now tell me, could you do it? Could you give him one of mine? I'd let you cut it off this minute—to-night, if you only would. If it would make him walk straight!"

Dudley seized hold of the doctor's coat excitedly, and Doctor Grant saw his whole soul was in his words.

"I'm afraid that would be an impossible feat, my boy. No—keep your own legs to wait upon him, and cheer him up all you can."

"Cheer him up!" was the fierce retort; "what could cheer him! I know he won't be able to live a cripple. He always says he is straight and upright though his chest is weak, and now when he knows it's no use trying to be strong any more, for he'll never be able to—when he knows he won't be able to play cricket, or football, or even climb the wall or run races—oh, it's awful—it will break his heart, and I wish I was dead!" After which passionate speech Dudley dashed away, and the doctor continued his walk shaking his head and muttering, "It's a bad lookout for the little fellow!"

Dudley ran across the lawn in his misery, and then nearly tumbled over Rob who was lying on the grass, his face hidden in his arms. He looked up and his eyes were red and swollen.

"Master Dudley, is it true, is he going to lose his legs?"

Dudley stood looking at him for a minute before he spoke, and then he said, "Yes, it's all that hateful doctor!"

Rob dropped his head on his arms again and a smothered groan escaped him.

Dudley continued his run out into the stableyard, from thence to the road, and he never stopped till he reached old Principle's little three-cornered shop.

Old Principle was busy serving customers when he came in; he gave him a friendly nod, and went on with his business whilst Dudley crept into the little back parlor, and sitting down in an old horsehair chair tried to recover his breath. It was not long before old Principle came after him.

"Well, my laddie," he said, laying his hand on the curly head, "there's sad news going through the village this morning, and I see by your face that 'tis true!"

Dudley nodded and then seizing hold of the old man's hand, leaned his head against it and burst into tears.

"Why does God do it!" he sobbed at length, "Roy is so much better than I am, he's always trying to please God, though he never talks about it, and I've prayed so hard that he might be made quite well!"

"Ay, and the good Lord is making him well perhaps though not by the way you planned. He might a been killed outright, and then what a trouble you'd have been in."

"This is nearly as bad," muttered Dudley.

"Now, laddie, don't harden your heart, are you one of the Lord's own children?"

"I don't know. I don't think I love God as much as Roy does."

"'Tis an awful bad principle," the old man continued, "to doubt and complain directly we can't understand the Almighty's dealings with us. He loves Master Roy better'n you and me, and the time will come when we'll thank the Lord with all our hearts for this accident."

This was utterly incomprehensible to Dudley.

"I feel very badly about it," old Principle went on, "and so do you, but the one I'm most sorry for is Ben Burkstone. I hear say he's fit to kill himself with despair!"

"Well," said Dudley, stopping his sobs for a minute; "I don't see it was his fault; it was the stupid pony; he funked it, and then fell and broke his knees; mine went over all right. Oh, why didn't it happen to me! If I had been spilled, I wouldn't have minded, and one leg wouldn't have been half so bad to me as to Roy!"

"I reckon you'd have got your leg all right again without having to lose it. 'Tis the laddie's delicate constitution that is so in his way. But I think you'll find Master Roy as plucky over the loss of his leg as he ever was. Now lift your heart up to God and ask Him that he may overrule it all for good. There goes the shop-bell!"

Old Principle disappeared, and Dudley soothed and comforted by his sympathy, retraced his steps to the house.

Meanwhile Miss Bertram had been going through the trying ordeal of breaking the news to the little invalid.

Roy was lying in bed, flushed and restless. His eyes looked unnaturally large and bright, as he met his aunt's anxious gaze.

"I'm so tired of pain, Aunt Judy, and I can't get to sleep."

Miss Bertram sat down and smiled her brightest smile.

Taking his thin little hand in hers she said tenderly,

"Yes, dear, you've been a brave little patient, but I hope you won't have much more to bear. You would like to be free from it, wouldn't you?"

"Am I going to die?"

"We hope you're going to get quite well again, if God wills, and if you will be a good boy and let the doctor cure you."

Roy's eyes were fixed intently on his aunt now.

"How are they going to cure me?"

Then Miss Bertram nerved herself for the occasion.

Amy Le Feuvre

"Roy, dear, you have been so patient since you lay here, that I know you will be patient over this. Doctor Grant says that your leg will never heal as it is, but he is sure you will get well and strong again if—if you will make up your mind to do without it."

"Does that mean he is going to cut it off?"

"Yes."

Dead silence, broken only by the flapping of the window-curtains in the breeze. Roy was not looking at his aunt now, but his eyes were fixed on the distant hills through the open window. A blackbird now hovering on some jasmine outside, suddenly lifted up his voice and burst into an exultant song. A faint smile flickered about Roy's lips.

"Do legs *never* grow again like teeth?"

The pathos of tone saved Miss Bertram from smiling at the comicality of the question.

"I'm afraid not, dear. Not until we reach heaven."

Then there was silence again, broken at last by Roy's saying in a very quiet tone,—

"I want to see Dudley."

Miss Bertram rose from her seat, but first she stooped to kiss him.

"You are quite a little hero," she said; "I will send David to you. My poor little Jonathan!"

A hot tear splashed on Roy's forehead; he put up his hand and stroked his aunt's face.

"Never mind, Aunt Judy, David made a better king than Jonathan would have I expect. Don't call Dudley just yet—I—I want to be alone."

Miss Bertram left him, but sat down outside his door on a broad window ledge and cried like a child.

And then a short time after, Dudley stole softly into the room and Roy's arms were clinging round his neck.

"Oh, Dudley, I've wanted you, kiss me!"

"You're going to get well, old chap, aren't you? You'll soon be out in the garden again."

Dudley was speaking in the gruff quick tones he used when trying to hide his feelings.

"We'll talk about that presently," said Roy, lying back on his pillows and making Dudley take a seat on his bed. "Dudley, do you know what a will is?"

"Yes; you've a strong will nurse always says."

"No, not that kind of one. Uncle James left a will when he died saying he left Norrington Court to father, and father left it to me. It's a piece of thick paper they write it down on, and it has some sealing wax on it. Aunt Judy showed me father's will once."

Dudley did not look enlightened, so Roy went on,—

"I want you to get a piece of paper and write down my

will for me. I will tell you what to say."

Dudley slipped out of the room obediently and returned with a sheet of note paper, but this did not satisfy Roy. "It must be a large sheet—very large," was his command.

After some minutes' search Dudley came in with a sheet of foolscap, and then with pen and ink he began to write at Roy's dictation:

"When I am dead"—

But Dudley's pen stopped. "You are not going to die, Roy?"

"I hope I am," was the unexpected reply; "I've been asking God to make me. I shouldn't think many people lived after their legs were cut off: I know I don't want to!"

"But I want you to live," cried poor Dudley; "oh! Roy you couldn't be so mean as to leave me all alone. Oh, do unsay that prayer of yours. You mustn't die!"

"I'm going to get quite ready to die," persisted Roy; "and if you really loved me you wouldn't think of liking to see me alive hopping about on a wooden leg, I couldn't do it."

"Nelson lived with only one arm," said Dudley.

Roy lay back on his pillows to consider this; then he said in a tired voice:

"Will you write what I want?"

Dudley seized the pen and in round, childish hand wrote as follows:

"When I am dead, Dudley is to have Norrington Court for his very own, and he is to live there instead of me. He can have Dibble and Nibble too. Rob is to have my musical box. I leave him my best tool box, and father's red silk pocket-handkerchief which I keep in the old tobacco pot on my chimneypiece. I leave granny her sovereign which she gave me, and my book 'Heroes of old England.' Aunt Judy is to have my best four-bladed knife, and my prayer book. I want old Principle to have my silver mug and my new writing case. I leave nurse the sovereign my guardian gave me to get herself some new shoes, and I leave her my Bible."

Thus far; then Roy gave a tired sigh. Dudley having entered completely into the spirit of the thing looked up and said eagerly, "There's your telescope, you know, Roy! If you leave it to me, I'll let you look through it when we're off on our travels."

"I shall never travel with no legs—besides I shall be dead. I'll leave my telescope to you."

Dudley subsided at once; then after a silence he asked meekly, "Is that enough?"

"Yes, I'm so tired, put—'I leave all my old clothes to the village boys, and my cricket bat and stumps to Ben'—but wait a minute, Dudley—there are all the servants, and I've got such heaps of books and toys—I think we'll leave it like that."

Dudley looked at his paper with some pride.

"I've only made six mistakes and three blots," he said; "now may I drop the sealing wax over it? I've got a lovely red piece in my pocket."

Amy Le Feuvre

"I think I have to write my name at the bottom first, I know father did. Give me the pen."

Dudley handed it, and wondered why Roy's fingers shook so as he signed his name.

"Is that all?"

"No, wait a moment. I want to write something myself."

And then in a large scrawl at the bottom of the paper Roy wrote—

"This boy died before he had time to serve the Queen, he tried to serve God, and he tried to do good to some people, only they turned out mistakes. He hopes the Queen will forgive him; he knows God will. Amen."

Dudley read this with awe.

"And is that a will?" he asked.

"Yes, let me drop some sealing wax; fetch a candle!"

Dudley was longing to do this part himself, but he generously said nothing, and presented Roy with a brass button out of his pocket, to stamp on the hot wax.

A lot of sealing wax was dropped indiscriminately all over the paper, and then old nurse appeared on the scene to order Dudley off.

"You've been far too long with him already, to my mind," she said; "if Miss Bertram wasn't beside herself she would never have given you permission at all; he ought to have been kept extra quiet, and he's worked himself all in a fever again." She put Roy gently back on his pillows, and did not notice in her short-sightedness the roll of paper being stuffed under his pillow. Dudley's spirits sank to zero, now he was about to be dismissed.

"Good-bye, Roy, ask to see me again, won't you?"

Roy held out his hand.

"I'll talk about it to-morrow," he said, faintly.

And Dudley crept out of the room feeling more forlorn and wretched than ever.

Amy Le Feuvre

X

A CRIPPLE

It was all over; two doctors had been closetted in the bedroom for a very long time, and then Dudley and Rob, sitting on the garden steps, were told that everything had been successfully carried out, and Roy was as well and better than had been expected.

"I never saw such fortitude and calm self-control in my life," said Miss Bertram to her mother; "it was unnatural for a child of his age!"

"He is a true Bertram in spirit," said the grandmother, proudly; then she added with a sigh, "but, alas, not in body."

"Nurse," said Dudley that night as he was creeping into bed under her charge; "is Roy going to die?"

"I hope not," answered nurse, a little tearfully. "Doctor Grant says he'll make a good recovery, but he whispered himself to me—Master Roy did just before he took the sleeping draught—'Nurse I'll have my leg buried with me!' he says."

Dudley was silent for a minute, then he asked, solemnly, "And where is it, nurse?"

Nurse turned upon him tearfully and angrily,

"I believe as how you haven't one speck of feeling for that blessed darling, you naughty boy! To talk of such a thing in such a way with not a tear on your face! And to think of him laying there a helpless cripple, and him the owner of the biggest estate in the county!"

Dudley crept into bed feeling he had no more tears to shed, wondering when he would be allowed to see Roy again, and also wondering who was the possessor of his lost leg.

It was a fortnight before he was allowed to see the little invalid, and when the boys met, Dudley gazed with deep pity on Roy's white little face, looking smaller and whiter than ever. But he welcomed him with a smile.

"It's years since you were here, old chap."

"Yes," responded Dudley, "and it's been the most miserablest years of my life."

"I thought I was going to die then," continued Roy, with still the same smile; "but God wouldn't let me. He was determined I should live, and do you know I've been thinking it out. I really believe it is because He is going to let me do something great still. And Doctor Grant has been telling me of a man in Parliament who took all the house by storm, and brought in a most wonderful law that thousands of people blessed him for, and he—he had a cork leg!"

Amy Le Feuvre

Certainly Roy had not lost his buoyancy of spirits. Dudley drew a deep breath of relief, and for the first time began to see brighter times ahead.

"And I'm going to have a cork leg," went on Roy, "a leg that if I press a spring I can kick out. Think of that!"

Dudley looked beaming, exclaiming,—

"And it will be very convenient to have a leg with no feeling, won't it, especially about the knee when you're crawling along a wall with broken bottles."

"I'm going to see Rob to-morrow," announced Roy, after a little more conversation. "Has he learned to read while I have been ill?"

Dudley shook his head.

"No, we tried one afternoon on the wall, but we were too miserable, so we stopped."

"Well, I can teach him here in bed. That's one thing you don't want a leg to do!"

"I say, Roy," Dudley asked, very cautiously; "don't you feel very funny without it?"

Roy looked away for a minute without answering, and then he said slowly:

"I try and not think about it. It will be worse when I get up—people might think when they see me in bed that I'm all right, but they'll know the truth when I'm up."

Then he added more cheerfully, "It's awfully queer, but do

you know I'd never know it wasn't there as far as the feeling goes. Why I can feel the pain right down to my toes now. And at night I'm always dreaming I'm running races with you as fast as I can, and then I wake and can't believe I'll never run again."

As Roy grew stronger he had more visitors; Rob came to him every day for a reading lesson, and old Principle brought him books and sweets. Ben was allowed an interview, and the old groom, with tears running down his cheeks, besought Roy to forgive him.

"I never ought to allowed you, and 'twas me that egged you on and sent you to your death!"

"No, it was my own fault, Ben," said Roy, humbly, "and the thing that pains me most—more than breaking my leg—is to think that I should be the first Bertram who has failed. Dudley did it, and I didn't, and of course I shall never be able to try it again. Perhaps I was too proud of what I could do. We have a picture in the nursery of a boy standing on the top of a bridge, and then tumbling in the water; it's called 'Pride must have a fall.' I've had a fall, haven't I, Ben?"

Ben came out from that interview declaring that "Master Roy ought to be sainted!"

One afternoon Rob was finishing his reading lesson when he looked up and said, a little shyly,

"Master Roy, you mind what you were a telling me of once—about what your father told you. Do you think as how I could do it too?"

"Of course you could, Rob. All of us ought to serve God."

Amy Le Feuvre

"I've been thinking a deal about it, and I should like to, if I knew how."

"Well, the Bible tells you. I remember nurse made me learn a text a long time ago, 'If any man serve me let him follow me.' It's just following Jesus I suppose, and doing what He wants us to do."

"How can we follow somebody we can't see?"

Roy knitted his brows. Rob's questions were hard to answer sometimes, and then a smile flashed across his face.

"I'll tell you. It's like this. On my birthday granny called me in to give me a birthday talk and, of course, she talked to me about my property. She said my uncle had managed it awfully well over there, and she hoped I would walk in his steps. That would be following him though he was dead, wouldn't it?"

"Ye-es," was the slow response.

"And so you see," Roy replied, leaning forward impress-sively, and his eyes glistening with earnestness, "we can each follow Jesus. Try and live as He did, and do and speak like Him. We read how He lived in the New Testament."

"And He was the one that died for us," Rob said, reflectively.

"Yes, He is the one you go to, to get your sins washed away. That comes first before we begin to serve Him."

"But I never could serve Him proper, always," objected Rob.

"No, nor more can any one. I'm awful, you know! Dudley says I think such a lot of myself. And of course Jesus never did. And I grumble and cry over my leg every day, and of course He wouldn't have done it. But Jesus forgives us again and again, and helps us to be good, and that's why we love Him, and because He died for us."

"Would He forgive me, and help me?" asked Rob; "are you quite sure He would care to have me for a servant?"

"Of course I'm sure. He wants everybody. You just ask Him."

Rob said no more. He was a lad of few words, and for some days did not touch on the subject again. His reading was progressing rapidly, and when Roy and Dudley found out that his birthday was near they laid their heads together and presented him with a handsome Bible, as they knew he was saving up his pennies to buy one.

His gratitude and delight overwhelmed them, and every day now, when his work was finished, he would sit down and spell out chapters of the gospels to himself.

As the days began to shorten, Roy grew so much stronger that he was able to be carried downstairs, and the first evening he was in the drawing-room, he asked Miss Bertram for the song of the two little drummer boys.

She sat down at the piano, and Dudley seeing Rob weeding a flower bed outside the open window, beckoned to him to come up closer and listen.

"It's the best song out," he shouted.

Roy's face shone as Miss Bertram's sweet voice rang

out triumphantly.

—"'the fight was won, and the regiment saved
By those two little dots in red!'"

"Oh, how I wish I could be a soldier!" was the muttered exclamation of Roy, "I shall never be able to serve the Queen now!"

"Nonsense," said Miss Bertram, briskly; "granny would tell you 'that all the Bertrams have always served the Queen, and only a few of them have been soldiers!'"

"Well, I suppose they have been sailors?" said Dudley.

"Not at all; we have only had one admiral, and three naval captains in our family during the last hundred years. Your father, Dudley, served the Queen as a governor in India quite as well as if he were fighting for her. Roy's father was her servant in Canada, though he had to do with politics; your uncle James served as a member of Parliament. The Queen has numbers of servants. I always think policemen are quite as brave as soldiers!"

"And what can a one-legged Bertram do?" Roy asked, with a pathetic smile that went straight to his aunt's heart.

"There's no reason why he shouldn't go into Parliament, and perhaps end by being a member of the cabinet."

"I never quite understand what that is," said Roy, contemplatively. "I don't think I should like to be shut up in a stuffy cupboard. They shut them up in it to talk, don't they, Aunt Judy?"

How Miss Bertram laughed! But whilst she was

explaining what a cabinet was, Rob crept away from the window muttering, "I suppose as how I could be a policeman, but I'd a deal rather be a soldier!"

Amy Le Feuvre

XI

A GIFT TO THE QUEEN

"Can I see Master Roy, please?"

It was Rob who spoke, and he seemed breathless with haste and importance, as he stood at the front door one cold afternoon the end of October.

"You can give me your message," the young footman said, rather superciliously.

"No, I can't," was the blunt retort; "ask Master Roy to speak to me."

Rob gained his point, and was ushered into the library where Roy and Dudley were amusing themselves in the firelight.

The old nursery was not much used now, and the library had begun to be considered the boys' room, partly because owing to it being on the ground floor, and opening into the garden, it was more convenient for Roy's use.

Roy was now the possessor of a cork leg; and with the help of a stick he was nearly as active as ever. His spirits were as high, and his purposes as plentiful as before his illness; and his grandmother and aunt marvelled that he could take his deformity so lightly. Yet there were times unknown to any, when Roy's brave little heart sank with the consciousness of it; and often in bed at night his pillow would be wet with tears.

"Oh, God," he would often pray, "you wouldn't let me die, do help me to do something worth living for. I feel my leg will keep away all the opportunities now, but please give me something big to do for you still."

"Hulloo, Rob, come on," was Roy's exclamation as he caught sight of his friend. "Just look at Nibble and Dibble, we're teaching them to draw a cart. It makes you die of laughing to look at them. There they go, and Dibble turns head over heels in his excitement!"

Roy's happy laugh rang out, but though Dudley joined him, Rob's face was grave and set.

"Please, can I speak to you on business, Master Roy?"

"Goody! What a long face!" exclaimed Dudley, pulling down his own in imitation of Rob's, and thereby causing a fresh peal of laughter from Roy. "Have you been a naughty boy, Rob, and has old Hal been thrashing you? Have you been skylarking on the top of the greenhouse, and smashed through on Hal's pate?"

"I should like to speak to Master Roy, alone," said Rob, a little wistfully; in no way disturbed by Dudley's teasing.

"Oh, it's one of your secrets again. I'll be off, Roy, I want to see old Principle!"

And Dudley dashed out of the room, whilst Rob came nearer and began his "business."

"Master Roy, I've been thinking a lot lately, and Miss Bertram asked me the other day if I'd like any other job for the winter as there's hardly enough work for me in the garden now. And yesterday I saw a chap in the village I used to know. He's a recruiting sergeant for the—shire regiment, and he wants me to enlist straight away. I wouldn't have given it a thought only what you said about serving the Queen has stuck to me, and it does seem a chance, and somehow that song has been in my head ever since I heard Miss Bertram sing it. I'd like to be in a regiment."

Rob paused for breath, and Roy's eyes were wide open with wonder and astonishment.

"But, Rob, you aren't old enough to be a soldier yet!"

"I'm just the age—they take them at eighteen, and I was that the other day, only I don't look it."

"But you're going to be my servant. I couldn't let you go."

Rob's face fell.

"I thought I could have seven years—or even twelve years would hardly find you ready to take up your property. And then I'd come back to you and never leave you again!"

"But I want you with me now—always"—said Roy, in a distressed tone; "I couldn't do without you all that time, and it's horrid of you to want to get away from here, I think."

"All right, Master Roy, I won't go—I'll get a job in the village that will keep me close at hand."

Rob tried to speak cheerfully, and after waiting a minute to see if Roy would say any more, he left the room quietly; all the light having died out of his honest grey eyes.

Roy watched the antics of his mice in the firelight, but his thoughts were far away from them. At last he opened the door and made his way up to his grandmother's room to have his usual chat with her before tea.

"Granny, if a person you like will do anything you like, ought you to make that person do what you like instead of what they like?"

"It sounds like a riddle," said Mrs. Bertram, with a smile. "I won't ask who the person is, the question is whether you like that person or yourself best. Which do you?"

Roy did not answer for a minute, then he hung his head.

"I'm afraid I like myself best."

"If you give me more details, perhaps I can advise you."

"Well, granny, may I talk first to Dudley about it, and then I'll tell you. But you see it's like this—the person wants to please you, and you can't pretend to be pleased if he does what doesn't please you!"

"I think the best plan would be to leave yourself out of the question entirely, and only think of the other person; that would be the most unselfish way."

Amy Le Feuvre

Roy knitted his brows and heaved a heavy sigh.

"Am I a very selfish person, granny?"

"You are much more selfish than Dudley is," said Mrs. Bertram, decidedly, who never minced matters with her grandsons.

Roy flushed a deep crimson, and his grandmother added,

"I do not say that you are altogether to blame, for Dudley has always given way to you and spoiled you; but you do not very often think of his wishes before your own."

"No, I never do."

Roy's tone was of the deepest dejection; but the sudden entrance of Dudley gave a turn to the conversation, and he gradually recovered his spirits.

When the two boys were at their tea half an hour later, Roy spread the whole matter before Dudley who looked at it in quite a different light.

"How stunning! And is he really going? Hurray! One of us will be a soldier, at any rate. I wish I was big enough to go with him."

"But I don't want him to go, and I told him so, and he isn't going!"

Dudley opened his eyes at this.

"You going to keep him back? Why you're the one that's always talking about serving the Queen, and fighting for her!"

"Yes, I should like to, but—but Rob is different. I want him to be with me."

"Then you don't care about serving the Queen, if you're going to do her out of a soldier who might fight for her!"

This was quite a new aspect of the affair.

"You think I'm like the dog in the manger? I can't go myself and I don't want him to. But if you go to a boarding school like Aunt Judy talks of, and I'm not allowed to go with you, and Rob is gone, I shall be left all alone; and I hate being alone, you don't know how I hate it—I think I should die!"

"Well, if I was you and knew I couldn't be a soldier myself, I would love to send some one instead of me—you know how they do in France. Old Selby was telling us. They pay a subsidy—substitute—don't you call it?—to go and fight for them."

"Yes, that is the coward's way," Roy said, scornfully.

He paused for a minute, and then his eyes flashed fire.

"Yes, Dudley, I'll let him go. It's me that's the coward to try and keep him back! You and I shall send him, and he shall be our substitute, and when we hear of him doing brave things, we shall feel it's ourselves. And we'll make him write letters to us and tell us all he is doing—oh, it will be splendid. How glad I am he has learned to read and write. Dudley, you just go and fetch him in, will you?"

Dudley crammed rather a large piece of cake into his mouth, and dashed out of the room; and a few minutes

Amy Le Feuvre

later dragged in the would-be soldier.

"We've settled you can go, Rob," said Roy, with a little of his masterful air about him; "only you're to go as *our* soldier. I think if I had had a good, broad, strong chest and never broke my leg, I should have enlisted, but you can go instead of me. Are you glad?"

"I'm sorry to leave you, Master Roy, but I'd dearly like to go."

"We must tell granny and Aunt Judy, and see what they say first. But I'm sure they'd like you to go."

No objection was made. Miss Bertram was rather pleased than otherwise.

"He will make a good soldier," she said, when talking it over with the boys; "he is a steady, reliable lad, with not too many ideas of his own, and implicitly obedient."

"Is that what makes a good soldier?" asked Roy. "I thought it was dash and bravery."

"Dash is a dangerous quality. Steady perseverance is better, Jonathan!"

The next few days were most exciting ones for the boys. Roy and Rob had many a long talk together, and very earnest and serious subjects were touched upon. Rob had little time left to bid his friends farewell, but he went to old Principle, as a matter of course.

"Yes," said the old man, a little proudly; "all the younger folks going out in life comes to me for a parting word. They laughs at me and my principles, but I'm proud of my nickname, and 'tis only right principles will make a man live right, and they knows it. What can I say to you, lad, but fear God and honor the Queen and those in authority under her. Never be afraid of holding to the right and denouncing the wrong, and may God Almighty take your body and soul in His keeping until we meet again."

Rob's last day came, and an hour before his departure, in company with his friend, the sergeant, he came up to the Manor to bid them all farewell. Roy had some farewell words with him in the privacy of his bedroom.

"We shall miss you awfully," he said, walking up and down the room to hide his emotion; "and it makes me wish I had your chance. But you'll remember, Rob, I look to you to be a rattling good soldier, much better than I should have been, and you'll be sure to do something grand and brave the very first opportunity, won't you? You must get the Victoria Cross, of course, and the account of you must be in the newspapers, so that we can read about you. And I shall pray that God will keep you safe, Rob. I hope you'll never have an arm or leg shot off, though I think that would be better than having them cut off. I hope you'll come back safe and sound. When shall we see you again?"

"The sergeant told me I should get a month or six weeks' leave this time next year, Master Roy."

"A year is a very long time. Rob, if I should die before I grow up, I want you to promise me that you will be Dudley's servant instead of mine. He will be master of Norrington Court, then, and I want you to live there."

"But you aren't going to die, Master Roy, you will live and do great things yet."

Roy shook his head a little sadly.

"Sometimes I wonder if I ever will. I won't give up trying, but I shall never be anything but half a man, with my cork leg and my weak chest. Dudley would make a much grander master. Still there's one thing I can do. I can serve God—and I've sent you to serve the Queen, and I can try to serve my fellow creatures. Good-bye, dear Rob, will you kiss me."

And then forgetting his dignity, Roy flung his arms round Rob's neck and hugged him passionately. "I'll never forget you carrying me home that night," he whispered in his ear, "I loved you from that time. And Rob you'll do what father told me to do—serve God first."

Rob nodded, and as he knelt on the ground holding the frail little figure to him, he made a promise there and then in his heart that he would never do or say anything that he would be ashamed of Roy's hearing.

"They're calling me, Master Roy, good-bye."

He was gone, and Roy sitting down on the floor, leaned his head against his bed and burst into tears.

Dudley found him there, and soon comforted him.

"Look here, if you like it, let us get upon the wall and see Rob and the sergeant drive by; we can just see the high road, and Rob had to go to the inn first, so we shall have plenty of time."

Roy's whole face beamed, he seized his stick and limped after Dudley without a thought of his leg, but when he reached the wall he came to a standstill.

"I'm afraid I can't climb it, Dudley, I've never been on it since my leg was broken!"

But Dudley would take no denial.

"Oh, yes, you can, I'll hoist you up, we'll manage it."

And "manage it" they did to Roy's intense delight, though Mrs. Bertram would have been horror-struck at the narrow escape the little invalid had, of falling to the ground during the proceeding.

When they saw the trap in the distance, they set up a wild cheer, and waved their handkerchiefs frantically, and when they were answered by a cheer and a fluttering piece of white, they felt quite satisfied at their farewell.

Before they got down from their high perch, Roy said, earnestly, "If God sent us Rob as an opportunity, Dudley, I wonder if we did him good."

"Well, you see he was such a lot bigger than us, and Aunt Judy says she never saw such a steady good boy; it's very difficult to do good to good people, because you want to be so extra good yourself."

"At any rate, we've made him the Queen's soldier."

"Yes," argued Dudley, provokingly; "but he was the first one that thought of it!"

"Oh, shut up," was Roy's impatient retort; "he told me himself it was the song of Jake and Jim that did it, and— and my talking to him."

"And I expect the sergeant thinks it's all his doing."

"But he wouldn't have gone unless I had told him he might."

And as usual Roy had the last word.

XII

LETTERS

Very disappointed were the boys at Rob's first letter, which arrived about a fortnight after he had gone to the regimental depot at a neighboring town.

"DEAR MASTER ROY:

"I hope you and Master Dudley are quite well as it leaves me at present. I like it first-rate, but it is hard work, and I have a good many masters, but I means to do my best. God bless you.

"From your faithful "ROB."

"That's not a letter at all!" said Roy, scornfully; "why he tells us nothing at all! Why he might have gone to school and told us more! That from a soldier. It's the stupidest rot I've ever heard!"

"I think you forget what a poor scholar Rob is," said Miss Bertram, reprovingly. "Now I think that is a remarkably good letter when I think what a short time he has been learning to write. You boys had better each write a proper letter to him yourselves, and ask him what you want to know. He will like to hear from you."

And so that afternoon, sitting up in state at the library table, the boys spread out their writing materials and began to write.

"I feel," said Roy, biting the end of his pen and looking up at the ceiling for an inspiration, "that I don't know quite how to begin. I should like to tell him not to write like an ass, when he knows he ought to tell us everything."

"All right, tell him so," said Dudley, squaring his elbow and frowning terribly as he prepared himself for the task. "You know what old Selby says: 'Make your paper talk, my boys, and make it talk in your own tongues.'"

After a great many interruptions from each other, and a few skirmishes round the table which resulted in the ink bottle being spilt, the letters were finished.

Roy read his aloud with pride to Dudley, who did the same to him.

"MY DEAR ROB:

"You must write us longer letters. I am quite sure there is lots to tell. What do you have to eat? And where do you sleep? Have you got a gun of your own? Do they let soldiers shoot rabbits on their half-holidays? Does the band play while you are at dinner? What are your clothes like, and what are you to be called, now you're a soldier? When will you be a sergeant, and is there any fighting coming off soon? Old Principle says you will be learning drill. What is drill? He says it's learning how to march, but Dudley and I can do that first-rate. How many masters have you got? Write to me to-morrow and tell me all. I hope you will remember you are our soldier, and be sure you do something very grand as quick as ever you can. Have you got a sword and a medal? Do you ride on a horse, and can you fire off the cannon? I miss you very much but you belong to us, and must come back full of glory.

"Your loving friend,

"FITZ ROY BERTRAM."

"MY DEAR ROB:

"I hope you like being a soldier. How many soldiers are there in the same house with you? Give them my love and tell them we hope they liked the cake we put in your box for them. Roy came down to old Principle's with me yesterday. He showed us a hammer out of his cave he dug up. He says you will not be a full blown soldier for a year. He had a cousin who was a sergeant in India—and had his brains burst out in battle. When do you begin to fight? Tell us if you feel funky, and what the enemy looks like, and who they are. We think you ought to write us a much jollier letter. Roy's leg is first-rate, and he is up on the garden wall now like a cat. We sit there to do our evening prep: for old Selby. Good-bye. We're on the lookout for your name in the newspapers the first battle that comes off.

"Roy's friend,

"DUDLEY."

"I don't think you've finished your letter properly," observed Roy, critically, as Dudley concluded reading his.

"Why do you write you're my friend?"

"Because I am," was the prompt reply; "I'm not Rob's friend and I shan't tell him I am. I just write to him because you do, that's all."

"Don't you like him?"

"I don't want him for my friend; he's going to be a kind of servant. Besides I wanted him to remember that I was your friend. I knew you long before he did, and if he was dead now, or if he never had been born, I should have been your friend just the same. We could have got on all right without him."

This was not the first touch of jealousy that had appeared in Dudley's character. He had more than once quarrelled with Roy on account of the boy who he said had crept in between them, but on Roy always emphatically assuring him that Rob occupied a back place in his affections, Dudley would generally be appeased and become his sunny self again.

"I like Rob very much," said Roy, slowly, "'specially now he's a soldier. I was thinking in church last Sunday, when they were reading about David and Jonathan, that Jonathan had an armor-bearer. That's Rob. Only I can't go to battle, so I send him. Don't you think that's a nice idea?"

"Did he get killed?" asked Dudley, with interest; "I forget about him."

"It doesn't say—I expect he lived as long as Jonathan did, and then perhaps David took him to be his servant. That's what I've settled with Rob, that he shall be your servant if

I die."

Dudley gave himself an impatient shake.

"Oh, shut up with that rot, you'll live as long as I do!"

Roy did not speak for a minute, then he said, slowly, "You remember my will that I made when I was so ill?"

"Yes, what did you do with it?"

"Aunt Judy found it the next morning on the floor nearly under the bed. She laughed a little at first, and then got quite grave when I explained it, and she took it away and locked it up somewhere. But if I never make another, you will remember that I have left Rob to you for your servant."

Dudley looked up with a comical gleam in his eye.

"And who gave Rob to you, old chap?"

"I took him—at least he gave himself to me."

Roy's tone was dignity itself, but Dudley laughed.

"Well he doesn't belong to you any longer; the Queen has got him."

"I have lent him to her, that's all."

"You talk of Rob as if he is a slave. He's a Briton, and 'Britons shall be free!'"

"So he is free, but he chose to be my servant when I grow up, and he shall be!"

Dudley dropped the argument, for Roy's face was flushing hotly, and he was wonderfully patient with him since his accident.

Miss Bertram entered the room at this juncture, and asked in her cheery brisk tones, "Would any boys like to drive me to the railway station in the pony trap? I am going up to London on business, and shall be away till to-morrow."

"Hurray," shouted Roy; "we'll come, and just read our letters, Aunt Judy! Won't they make Rob see how he ought to write?"

Miss Bertram took the letters in her hand, praised the little writers, and then sent them off to their rooms to get tidy for their drive.

A short time after, Roy mounted in front with his aunt, was driving her with pride along the high road; whilst Dudley from the back seat kept them lively with his chatter and flow of fun.

The boys always liked the bustle of the station; and getting a lad to hold the pony, they followed their aunt to the platform and saw her on board the train. Some friends spoke to her before the train went off and amongst them was a certain Captain Smalley.

"I say," said Dudley, nudging Roy; "he's an officer, and he is in the army, I expect he knows Rob."

"We'll ask him, directly the train is off."

But in the bustle of the last few minutes they missed seeing him; the young captain got into his dog-cart, and was well on his way home before the boys were ready to start in their trap.

"Oh, I say! See him in the distance! Whip up and let us catch him. Here, let me drive, it's my turn now!"

But Roy clutched hold of the reins.

"No, I want to."

"I tell you it's my turn!"

"It's the only thing I can do with one leg, it's a beastly shame of you!"

Dudley, who had nearly got possession of the coveted reins dropped them instantly.

"All right then, but go ahead!"

And then Roy with a shamed look put the reins in his cousin's hands.

"I'll give them up. Granny always says I'm selfish. It was awfully mean to talk of my leg. Now then hurry! Gee-up!"

Dudley took the reins with a gratified smile, applied the whip, and the spirited little pony dashed along the road at such a rate, that a porter looked after them in dismay.

"Those two young gents will come to their death afore they're satisfied," he remarked, and another man responded:

"Yes, the little one is pretty well smashed up already, but legs or no legs, boys allays keeps their sperrits!"

Amy Le Feuvre

Captain Smalley was rather startled at hearing frantic shouts behind him, and when he pulled up wondering if some message were to be delivered, he was still more bewildered by what he heard.

"Hi, Captain Smalley! Stop for us. We've come two miles out of our way. Now then, Roy, go ahead!"

"Do you know Rob? We want you to tell us how he is. We can't get a word out of him; is there going to be any fighting? And how does he look in his clothes?"

"Who is Rob?" asked Captain Smalley.

"Why, he's a soldier like you. You must know him!"

A few more explanations were made, and then the young man laughed heartily.

"Your young friend is learning his recruit drill at the depot, I should think. If he were in my regiment I might not be able to give you much information about him. The army is a big affair, my boys, and I doubt if Rob and I will ever meet."

The boys' faces fell considerably.

"Do you think he likes it?" asked Roy, anxiously; "do you like being a soldier?"

"Of course I do, and if he has any stuff in him he will like it, too."

"And will he be sent to fight very soon?"

"I dare say he may do his seven years without a

single fight!"

Roy looked very disappointed.

"If he doesn't fight, he might just as well have stopped at home. What's the good of being a soldier if you don't have any battles?"

"Soldiers prevent battles, sometimes."

This sounded nonsense to the boys. They bade the captain good-bye, and turned their pony's head homeward quite disconsolate.

"I'll write and tell him to come home if he's not going to do anything," said Roy, with his little mouth pursed up determinedly.

"We'll give him a chance, first. He may go out to fight. Captain Smalley didn't say for certain."

"I think Captain Smalley is funky himself about fighting, that's what I think!"

And with this disdainful assertion Roy dismissed the subject.

Amy Le Feuvre

XIII

OLD PRINCIPLE

It was a soft, mild day in December. Mr. Selby's study seemed close and stifling to the boys as they sat up at the long table with books and slates before them, and a blazing fire behind their backs.

"This sum won't come right, Mr. Selby," groaned Roy; "and I've gone over it three times. It is made up of nothing but eights and nines. I hate nine. I wish it had never been made. Who made up figures, Mr. Selby?"

Roy's questions were rather perplexing at lesson time.

"I will tell you all about that another time," was Mr. Selby's reply. "Have another try, my boy: never let any difficulty master you, if you can help it."

A knock at the door, and Mr. Selby was summoned to some parishioner. He was often interrupted when with his pupils, but they were generally conscientious enough to go on working during his absence.

But Roy's lesson this morning was not interesting, and he was unusually talkative.

"It's no good trying to master this sum, it's all those nines. They're nasty, lanky, spiteful little brutes, I should like to tear them out of the sum-books."

"Expel them from arithmetic," said Dudley, looking up from a latin exercise, his sunny smile appearing. "Don't you wish we could have a huge dust hole to empty all the nasty people and things in that we don't like?"

"Yes—I'd shovel the nines in fast enough, and a few eights to keep them company, and then I would throw in all my medicine bottles, and my great coat, and—and Mrs. Selby on the top of them!"

This last clause was added in a whisper, for if there was any one that Roy really disliked, it was his tutor's wife. She was a kind-hearted woman, but fidgety and fussy to the last degree, and was always in a bustle. Having no children, she expended all her energies on the parish, and there was not a domestic detail in any village home that escaped her eye. She had spoken sharply to the boys that morning for bringing in muddy footprints, and her words were still rankling in Roy's breast.

"It's so awfully hot," Roy continued; "let us open the window, Dudley. Old Selby won't mind for once; it's like an oven in here."

The window was opened with some difficulty, and the fresh air blowing in seemed delicious to the boys. Roy clambered up on the old window-seat, slate in hand, but his eyes commanded the view of the village street, and the sum made slow progress in consequence.

"I say! Tom White's pig has broken loose, and that stupid Johnnie Dent is driving it straight into old Principle's! I expect he'll come out in an awful rage. No—the door must be shut, he can't get in. There seems quite a crowd round old Principle's. He's giving them a lecture, I expect. Here comes old Mother Selby tearing up the street, her bonnet strings are flying and she's awfully excited!"

A minute after the door was thrown open.

"John, it's the most extraordinary thing—oh, you are not here!—Where is Mr. Selby? I always knew something would happen to that old man roaming over the hills half the night, and digging holes big enough to bury himself! John! Where are you?"

She disappeared as quickly as she had come, banging the door violently behind her; but Roy sprang down from his seat instantly.

"Dudley, it's old Principle! Something must have happened to him, do let us go and see."

Dudley dashed down his pen, and was vaulting out of the window, when he suddenly stopped.

"Roy get your great coat, quick. Aunt Judy made me promise to look after you. I'll wait while you get it."

Roy dashed out into the hall. He heard the rector's voice in the distance, but was too excited to wait to see him, and after impatiently tugging on his objectionable coat, he limped off as quickly as he could, joining Dudley at the garden gate. They heard the news on the way to old Principle's. It appeared that the old man had gone out the afternoon before, and had never come home. His shop was shut up exactly as he had left it, and the woman who went in every day to do his cleaning and cooking for him, was the first one to notice his absence. The group of idle women round his door were busily discussing the question when the boys arrived.

"I shouldn't be a bit surprised if as how he has made away with hisself," suggested one, knowingly. "I always did say as he were queer in the head, a makin' out of a pack o' stones such amazin' stories! And a mutterin' to hisself like no ordinary creetur, and a walkin' through the woods and fields as if he seed nothin' but what other folks couldn't see at all!"

"Ah, now! To think of it! And Bill is a goin' down the river to find his body; for him and Walter Hitchcock have searched the whole place since seven o'clock this mornin'!"

"May be there's a murder in it," said a young woman, cheerfully. "He were an old man to wander off alone, and there's allays evil-doers round about for the unprotected."

The boys listened to these and similar conjectures with frightened eyes; then Dudley whispered,

"I believe he is in his cave, Roy; we'll go and look for him. Only don't tell these women about it, because he hasn't told anybody but us where it is."

They left the shop and started for the hills, but Roy's lameness made progress very slow.

At last he stopped, and struggling to hide his disappointment said, "You'll have to go on without me, Dudley. I only keep you back. This old leg of mine always comes in the way."

Amy Le Feuvre

Dudley stopped to consider. "It's a very long way, but we must get there somehow. Hulloo, here's just the thing."

They had stopped at a small inn at the outskirts of the village; and tied to the drinking trough outside, was a rough pony and cart whose owner was enjoying himself in the tap room with his friends.

"Jump in, Roy. It's to save old Principle, and anybody would be glad to lend his cart for that."

Roy was not long in acting upon this advice. The pony trotted forward briskly, and the boys would have thoroughly enjoyed this escapade, except for the fears of their friend's safety.

"If anything has happened to him, the village will go to the dogs!" Roy asserted, emphatically; "old Hal said the other day he was worth a couple of parsons. When I grow up, I think I shall try and be like him. I shall give good advice to everybody without ever scolding them, that is what he does."

"Do you think he is dead?" asked Dudley, "I don't think he can be. Why it was only the day before yesterday we saw him, and he was as well as we are."

It seemed a long time before they reached the cave; the hills were steep and the pony rather old, and more than once Dudley felt inclined to run forward on his own two legs. Roy at last suggested this.

"I can drive up after you as fast as I can; and if you find him you holloa to me."

So Dudley jumped out and was soon lost to sight behind

the bushes and hollows that fringed the hills.

Roy drove on busily thinking, and wondering if they had done wisely to take the matter into their own hands, and come off alone as they had done.

When he at length reached the cave Dudley came to meet him with a puzzled face.

"Something has happened, Roy. I can't get into it very far; there's a lot of earth tumbled down and I can't move it."

"Then old Principle is buried alive!" cried Roy in terror. "Quick, Dudley, let us dig him out."

Dudley seemed quite helpless.

"I've no spade, and there's no place near to get one. I wish we hadn't come alone."

This was a dilemma, but Roy would not be overcome by it.

"Let us look about for his tools; he always brings them up with him. Isn't there enough room for me to get in, Dudley?"

Dudley shook his head, and both boys approached the entrance. There had indeed been a serious landslip, and it was impossible to remove the great blocks of stone and earth that had fallen without proper tools; and though they searched for some traces of old Principle, not a thing belonging to him could they find.

"Perhaps he may not be here."

"I believe he is," maintained Roy; "and we must be as quick as ever we can. Dudley you go back in the cart and get some men to come and help. I will stay here. How I wish we hadn't come alone!"

Left by himself, Roy did not sit down and do nothing. Clambering all amongst the fallen earth and stone, he eagerly searched for some crevice or opening; and at last high up in the ravine he found one. Then lying down flat on the ground he put his mouth to the hole. "Old Principle! Hi! Old Principle! Are you there?"

It was not fancy that a muffled voice came up to him—

"Help! I'm here!"

That gave Roy fresh strength. Eagerly he tore aside brambles and stones with small thought of his scratched, bruised hands, and at last had the satisfaction of viewing a hole big enough to drop his slim little body through. Then he called again,

"Old Principle, I'm coming down from the top. Are you hurt? Can you tell me if it is far to fall?"

And this time old Principle's voice sounded clearer:

"God help you, laddie! For I can't help you or myself. No it is not a very big drop from where you are."

For one moment Roy looked at the dark chasm below him with hesitation, then he murmured to himself, "If I break my other leg, I must get to him—poor old Principle."

And then carefully and cautiously he let himself down, clinging with his hands to a stout twig of mountain ash that bent and swayed across the crevice with his weight.

Another moment and leaving go of the friendly branch, he dropped on damp fresh soil, and found himself in almost total darkness. Then as his eyes got more accustomed to it, he saw the prostrate form of old Principle only a yard or two away from him. The old man was breathing heavily, and his legs were completely buried under fallen earth.

"Is it Master Roy?" he said, as Roy came over and took hold of his hand; "ay, you shouldn't have imprisoned yourself with me, laddie—I didn't rightly think of what you were doing—I'm—I'm in such pain!"

"Are you very hurt? Oh, dear, what can I do? I can't lift you. Are your legs broken?"

"I don't rightly know. If you could shift a little of the earth off, may be it would ease me!"

Roy looked round and then delightedly seized hold of a small shovel.

"Your shovel is here. I'll do it," he said, cheerfully, and then to work he went. The soil was fortunately not heavy to remove, but there was a great quantity of it before poor old Principle's legs were liberated. Roy toiled on, hot and breathless, longing that help should come, his own fatigue forgotten in his pity for the helpless old man.

"Can you lift yourself up, old Principle? I really think I've got the earth off your legs—at least most of it!"

There was a struggle, then a groan.

"I'm afraid not, laddie. 'Tis the power that has quite gone out of them. I'm fearing that old Principle will be never roaming the hills again, but there 'tis the Lord's will, and He never do make mistakes."

"Do you think your legs are broken like mine were?"

"I can't rightly say. It has seemed a weary time since I lay here. Many days and nights I suppose—and I'm longing for a drink, but thank the Lord, He has sent you to me."

"It is only since yesterday that you have been lost. And Dudley has gone back to get some men to come. I wish I could get you some water, but there's none here, is there?"

"I am afraid not."

Silence fell on the pair, which was broken at last by,—

"'Tis a good principle to think of your mercies when trouble overtakes you. It has whiled away the time here, and I can thank the Lord with all my heart, that my head and hands are uninjured!"

"How did it happen?" asked Roy.

"I'm afraid I excavated too far and was in the midst of unearthing a large boulder of stone when I remembered no more—it took me so sudden, and when I came to life again I thought I was in my bed at home with a ton's weight on my feet. 'Twas good of the Lord to give me air—that crevice you came through has saved me."

"You said a long time ago you could mend anything but broken hearts, but you can't mend broken legs, can you? Or you would have mended mine."

"Ay, ay, so I would, surely. No—the mender has turned into a breaker this time, 'tis a good thing it's only himself that he has broken up."

A slight groan escaped him, and Roy softly stroked his face, a broken sob escaping him.

"Oh, old Principle, how I wish I was strong, how I wish I could move you! You aren't broken up! Don't say you are. Couldn't I help you to roll over on your back, wouldn't that be better?"

After great effort this was partly accomplished, and then to Roy's intense relief he heard voices above.

Running to the opening he shouted:

"Here we are! Help us out, or old Principle will die!"

But it was some time before the rescue could be accomplished. The opening was small enough to let Roy through, but not old Principle, and the boy refused to leave the old man. Pickaxes and shovels were set heartily to work, and after half an hour's hard toil, the old man was gently raised out of his dangerous position, and placed in the cart. Roy was put in with him, and Dudley walked by the side in silence until they reached the village. There was a great stir and excitement over their return. Mrs. Selby and their aunt met the boys at the entrance of the village, and Miss Bertram looked anxiously at Roy's little white set face.

He could not be torn away from his old friend till he heard the doctor's verdict, and it was a far more hopeful one than anybody had anticipated.

Amy Le Feuvre

"It is a marvellous escape. Not a bone broken, but of course he is terribly bruised and shaken, and very stiff."

"I'll sit with him till we can get a proper nurse," said good-natured Mrs. Selby; "he seems to have no kith or kin belonging to him. It will be a lesson to him, for life, I hope, and will put a stop to all this delving and digging and unearthing what is best left alone. It only fosters scepticism in the minds of the ignorant, and teaches them to disbelieve their Bibles!"

Old Principle looked up with a smile after the doctor's visit.

"Is little Master Roy there?"

Roy pressed forward eagerly.

"I'm thinking, laddie, that you and Master Dudley have had a rare good opportunity of saving a poor old man's life, and he is duly grateful to you."

But Roy was very near tears.

"I'm so glad—so glad your legs aren't broken," he said, in a quivering voice, "anything is better than being suddenly turned into a cripple!"

And then bending over him he kissed the furrowed brow, and crept out of the room.

XIV

HEROES

Old Principle's accident was a great event in the village. The boys got their fair share of praise in his rescue, but their grandmother did not see it in such a favorable light.

"You ought never to have left your lessons without leave, or taken a cart belonging to a stranger all unknown to him, or gone off alone without telling any one about it. And you were shown the folly and uselessness of such a proceeding by arriving on the scene and being utterly unable to extricate him from his position. If children would realize their weakness and foolishness more in these days, they would develop into better men and women, but self-sufficiency and self-conceit are signs of the times!"

Every day the boys went to see their friend, and even Mrs. Selby allowed that they could be quiet and well-behaved in a sick room. It was a long time before old Principle regained his health, and he seemed to have grown much older and feebler since his accident; but his serenity of spirit was undisturbed, and some of the neighbors who had before voted him close and cranky, now offered to come and sit with him, and learned many a lesson from

Amy Le Feuvre

his sickbed. When he was at last able to take his place in the shop again, Roy's mind was at ease about him.

"I was so afraid he was going to die as long as he stayed in bed," he confided to Dudley: "I hope no one will ever die that I like, it must be such a dreadful thing to have them gone. I think I would rather die first, wouldn't you?"

"We can't all die first," said matter-of-fact Dudley; "some-body must be last."

"Well, I don't think I shall be," returned Roy, "that's the best of being weak like I am."

But this assurance brought no comfort to Dudley.

A few more labored letters came from Rob, and then one that stirred the boys' hearts after he had been about three months away from them. It was to say that he was going out to India in a draft, and had been allowed three days to come and say good-bye to his friends.

Roy was almost beside himself with excitement at the prospect of seeing him again; and when the day came, he insisted upon going to the station by himself to meet him. Dudley perched on the garden wall awaited their coming.

Rob was certainly improved in appearance. He held him-self up bravely, but a softened light came into his eyes, as Roy, looking whiter and more fragile than ever, flung himself into his arms, utterly regardless of all onlookers.

"I'm right glad to see you, Master Roy," said Rob, in a husky voice.

"Oh, Rob, you look so splendid! And you've got to be

quite a man! Come on, I'm going to drive you home, and we shall be all by ourselves. Now tell me, are you really and truly happy?"

Rob did not answer this question till he was in the trap being driven homeward; then he said, slowly, "Yes, I'm thinking I like it first-rate, but 'tis hard in many ways. 'Tis hard to keep straight and do the right, when most seems to live the other way."

"But most of the soldiers aren't bad, are they?" questioned Roy with startled eyes.

"They aren't out and out bad—just careless, I reckon, but old Principle would say they're lacking in principle."

"And is it hard being a soldier? I suppose it must be a little. I came across a text I thought would just fit you, Rob, the other day. 'Endure hardness as a good soldier of Jesus Christ.'"

Rob's eyes brightened. He seemed strangely older and graver in his ways, yet when they drove up in sight of Dudley who slipped down over the wall, and tumbled himself into the trap with them, he made the boys roar with laughter with his funny incidents of barrack-room life.

The three days passed only too soon. Innumerable were the questions put to the young soldier, and Roy's curiosity about a military life was insatiable.

"Well," he said at last, "I don't think I should be strong enough to be a soldier, but I'm awfully glad you're one, Rob. And now you've got your chance in India of doing something grand and getting the Victoria Cross. The opportunity has come to you, and Dudley and I can't get it, though we've tried hard. But we have helped to send you out to India to do it, Rob, so you won't fail us, will you? And then when you come back covered with medals, you shall live with me and always dress in your uniform, so we'll look forward and think of that!"

When Rob departed, he had quite a little party of friends to see him off at the station. Old Hal, the gardener, Ted, the stable-boy, and old Principle were there, and Miss Bertram and her nephews were with him to the last.

"He's begun right, and he'll go on like it," announced old Principle, with emphasis, as the train steamed out of the station, and Rob leaned out of the window to wave a last farewell to his friends. "'Tis the beginnin' of life that boys make such a mess of, as a rule!"

Roy's eyes were tearful as he watched the train disappear.

"I've given him to the Queen," he said, gravely, to his aunt; "and no one can say I'm selfish, for I'd much rather have had him stay with me. But as I can't do anything grand, he must do it for me!"

The day after Rob left them, the boys had an invitation to spend the day with Roy's guardian, General Newton. He did not often ask them over to see him, so it was considered a great treat, and they set off in high spirits. The groom drove them over, and they were shown into the general's study at once upon their arrival. He was not by himself; another grey-haired gentleman was seated there smoking, and the boys wondered at first who he was, but General Newton soon enlightened them.

"This is a very old chum of mine, boys, who was in my

regiment with me when I first enlisted; he has been a hero in his time, so if you make up to him he will tell you some wonderful stories. Now, Manning, these boys are smitten with the 'scarlet fever' at present, as a young friend of theirs has just enlisted. Tell them something about the Crimea; you had plenty of ghastly experiences there."

Colonel Manning laughed as he met the boys' admiring gaze, and before long he was enchanting them by his reminiscences.

"Now will you tell us the very bravest thing that you ever saw any soldier do?" demanded Roy, with flushed cheeks and sparkling eyes.

Colonel Manning looked at his little auditor rather thoughtfully.

"I've seen a good many brave deeds done," he said, slowly; "but one stands out in my memory above and beyond them all."

"Oh, do tell us."

"It was quite a young lad, a recruit that came to join our regiment when we were in Malta. He was a fair, curly-headed boy, and seemed quite frightened at the rough life and ways of his comrades. I happened to be orderly officer one evening, and was going my rounds, when I passed one of the barrack-rooms just before lights were out. It was in a low building and the windows were open. The men were noisy, and the first thing I heard was a volley of oaths from one of the oldest soldiers there. The corporal in charge instead of reproving him, was joining in, and there was a great dispute between a lot of them about some small matter, when this young chap stood up

Amy Le Feuvre

with a flush on his cheeks. 'Comrades,' he cried; 'would any of you allow your mother to be called evil names in the barrack-room?' His voice rang put so clearly that there was a hush at once, and they turned to him in wonder. 'You know you wouldn't,' he went on; 'and you are ill-treating the name of One who is dearer and nearer to me than any mother—the best Friend I've got. I tell you, I won't allow you to do it while I am in the room!' I remember as I stood there and heard him, and saw the men utterly abashed before the boy, I felt he had a courage that none of us could equal."

"Is that all?" asked Dudley, with disappointment in his tone.

"Did the men stop swearing?" asked Roy.

"As far as I can remember, they did. The corporal rebuked them, and lights were put out, but that boy was braver than many a hero on the battlefield."

The boys' faces fell.

"But that was not what we call a brave deed," said Roy, at length. "Of course it was splendid of him, but it wouldn't get him the Victoria Cross."

"No, only a crown of everlasting life, and a word of commendation from the King of Kings," said the colonel, in a strangely quiet voice; but Roy's expressive little face kindled at once, and he said no more. They went into the dining-room to lunch soon, and the boys were too busy enjoying the good things before them to talk much to their elders. After it was over General Newton sent them out for a run in the garden. And then when they came in, he asked them if they would like to come upstairs to his old picture gallery.

"I am going to take my friend up, and you can come, too."

The boys were delighted; they had often heard of this gallery, but had never been in it as General Newton kept it locked up, and very rarely opened it.

"I have some gems amongst the portraits," he said to Colonel Manning as he unlocked a door in the passage, and led them into a long dusky corridor; "I will pull up the blinds and then we shall see. They are mostly ancestors, but one or two are by master hands, and two or three royal personages are amongst them."

The boys listened eagerly whilst their host pointed out one and another, with now and then an anecdote connected with them.

"Look," said Roy, delightedly, "there's a fine soldier. He is quite young, and yet what a lot of medals! and oh, General Newton, isn't that the Victoria Cross on his coat?"

"Yes, my boy, he served his country well for such a youngster, he fought in eight battles, and came home without a scratch, though he had many hair-breadth escapes. In one battle he had two horses shot under him, and he saved the colors on foot, though he was leading a cavalry charge."

"He was a regular hero!" murmured the admiring boys.

"I don't think he was," said the general, drily. "He had plenty of dash and go, but no moral courage. He came home after the wars were over, and broke his mother's

Amy Le Feuvre

heart by becoming a drunkard and a gambler; and he died an early death from drink and dissipation."

Roy looked very puzzled.

"I thought a brave man must be a good one, and brave and good to the end of his life."

"A man can face the cannon's mouth better than a friend's ridicule," said General Newton; "the young soldier we were hearing about before dinner had a nobler courage than this poor fellow here."

Roy said no more, but though he listened and looked, the rest of the time they were in the gallery, his thoughts were with the hero of the Victoria Cross. He ran back to have one more look at him before they went downstairs, and gazed up at the bold, frank bearing, and the laughing mouth of the soldier, with wistful pity in his brown eyes.

"You served your Queen and country, but I expect you left out God," he said, in a whisper; then he ran on to overtake the others.

After an early tea the boys were packed up in the trap to come home.

"Drive home as quickly as you can," said the general to the groom, "for rain is not far off, and it will not do to let Master Fitz Roy get a soaking; he looks as if a breath of wind will blow him away."

"I do hate people talking about me like that," Roy confided to Dudley as they set off at a brisk rate; "I might just as well be a girl. I often wonder I wasn't born one for all the good that I shall do in the world."

"That's all stuff," said Dudley, indignantly; "you'll be an awfully strong man I expect when you grow up, you see if you aren't!"

Roy shook his head, and was unusually silent for some time. They were driving through the outskirts of a village when down came the rain. The groom wrapped the boys up as well as he could, and was urging the horse on, when it suddenly shied and came to a standstill. Looking down, the groom saw a small child seated in the middle of the road, almost miraculously preserved from the horse's hoofs.

"Well, here's a go," he muttered; "where on earth does it come from, we don't want no delay in such a storm as this!"

The boys had sprung down at once from the trap, and were endeavoring to drag the child away when it burst into roars of fright and anger.

"I want mummy—oh, mummy!"

It was a little girl between three and four. She had been placidly nursing a doll in the middle of the road, and seemed perfectly oblivious of wind and rain.

"Where do you live?" asked Roy, but the child only continued to wail for its mother.

"Here, Master Roy, you'll be wet through. Come back, and let Master Dudley hoist her up to me. We can't stop all day trying to find out where she lives. We'll take her back with us for the time."

But this did not please Roy.

"No, we must find her mother; she must come from the village we have passed. You wait there with the horse, Sanders, and we'll take her back."

"Let Master Dudley do it, then," said Sanders, crossly, "and you get into the trap again."

This also Roy refused to do.

"It's an opportunity, isn't it, Dudley? And look she has taken hold of my hand; you run on in front and ask about her at the first cottage you come to, and I'll bring her after you."

Sanders grumbled and growled, but the boys did not heed him. Happily the mother of the child soon appeared, thanked them profusely, and Roy and Dudley clambered up into the trap again, both wet through.

"You're a heedless, disobedient pair," said the wrathful Sanders, "and if I'm blamed for your taking to your beds and gettin' rheumaticky fever and inflammation of the lungs, it won't be my fault, and I shall tell the missus so!"

XV

AN UNWELCOME PROPOSAL

Roy was not well for some time after this episode. He had a bad bronchial attack, and was in the hands of his old nurse again.

"It do seem as if everything conspires to make you a delicate lad," she said one day; "it beats me how you come through it as well as you do! But 'tis mostly your thoughtless ways that leads you into trouble."

"I'm sorry," Roy said, cheerfully; "but I expect I'm stronger than I look. I never shall be much of a fellow, I know; but even with my cork leg I can do a good deal, can't I?"

"You're worth two of Master Dudley!" ejaculated the fond nurse, but this assertion was of course questioned.

"I shall never be like Dudley, never! Not in looks, or strength, or goodness. He is better than I am all round!"

Miss Bertram came into the room at this moment.

"Ah, nurse," she said, in her bright, brisk way; "he is like

Amy Le Feuvre

a cat, isn't he? Has nine lives, I'm sure. There never was such a boy for getting into scrapes. I'm in fear whenever he is out of our sight now that he may never come back again."

"Now, Aunt Judy, you wouldn't have liked me not to have got out to that baby?"

"I should like some one else to have done it."

"Yes, I suppose Dudley would have done it," and Roy's tone was a little sad; "but you see I wanted to help. As he was saying to me this morning, he will have many more chances than I when he gets bigger and goes out to India to do good to people. I shall have to stop at home now, for I shall never be able to ride, he will have all the big opportunities, and I must be content with the little ones."

"You talk like a little old grandfather, sometimes," said Miss Bertram, laughing, as she sat down beside him. "You must make the most of David while he is with you, for I have heard from his stepfather this morning, and he wishes him sent to school at once."

Roy's eyes opened wide.

"But I shall go too, shan't I, Aunt Judy?"

"I am afraid not just yet. You are not fit to rough it; besides we couldn't lose both our boys!"

"But I must go if Dudley goes, I must!" and Roy's tone was passionate now. "I won't have him go away from me—I've lost Rob, and that is bad enough—You wouldn't take Dudley away from me, too, Aunt Judy!"

"Hush, hush, we will not talk any more about it now. He will not go till after Easter, and that won't be here yet."

Miss Bertram was sorry she had broached the subject, when she saw Roy's distress, and going downstairs sent Dudley up to play with him.

Later on when she was sitting with her mother in the drawing-room a small head appeared. "May I come in, granny?"

It was Dudley, and his round and rosy face was unusually solemn. Marching in he took up his position on the hearth-rug, his back to the fire, and with his hands deep in his pockets, he turned his face rather defiantly toward his grandmother.

"Granny, I'm not going to school without Roy."

"Hoighty-toity! What next, I wonder. Is that the way for little boys to speak to their elders. You will do what you are told as long as you are in my house, as your father did before you."

"It is your stepfather's wish," put in Miss Bertram; "you ought to be willing to obey him."

"Not if he tells me to do something wrong. And I'm sure it would be quite a wrong thing for me to go away from Roy. We have promised never to leave each other till we grow up, and we don't mean to break our promise. And, granny, I'm sure you don't like broken promises. Father doesn't know about Roy, and he can't understand like I do, and it would be very wrong of him if he took me away from Roy!"

Amy Le Feuvre

Mrs. Bertram put on her glasses and inspected her little grandson with searching eyes.

"That is a most disrespectful speech, Dudley. I shall of course uphold your father's wishes."

"But, granny, I can't leave Roy. It will break his heart. You don't know how he frets about his leg. He doesn't say much and is always so cheerful, but he misses me most awfully even if I'm away for a day. If he was well and strong, he could get on first-rate, but he wouldn't get about half so much if I didn't take him. I think he would mope and mope all by himself. And I don't think we could live without each other. You won't send me away, will you?"

Tears were filling Dudley's blue eyes, but Mrs. Bertram looked displeased.

"In my days, children never thought of arguing with their elders. I think your aunt and I are as capable of taking care of Roy as you are. Now leave the room, and do not refer to the matter again."

Then Dudley astonished his grandmother by the first exhibition of temper that he had ever displayed before her.

"I *won't* be separated from Roy. If you send me to school, I shall run away, and I shall write and tell father the reason!"

A stamp of the foot emphasized this passionate speech, and then Dudley fled from the room, banging the door violently behind him.

As on a former occasion he now took himself and his grief to old Principle. It was early-closing day in the village, and he found the old man just locking up his door prepared for a ramble.

"Come along up to the hills with me, laddie," he said, after hearing the trouble; "there's nothing like fresh air for blowing away a fit of the dumps. I am going to the cave again—will you come with me?"

"Yes, I will. I've been in an awful temper in granny's room, and banged her door. I don't think she'll ever forgive me!"

"'Tis like this, Master Dudley," said old Principle, presently, as they walked over the hills together; "if it's right for you to go, there's nothing to be said, and you must fall in with it whether you like it or no."

"But it can't be right for me to leave Roy when he wants me."

"It may be the best thing in the world for him and you, if it is to be. 'Tis a bad principle to determine whether a thing is right or wrong, according to our liking."

"It's a cruel thing to part us!" said Dudley, doggedly.

"But may be a way will be found out of the difficulty by Master Roy going with you."

"They say he isn't strong enough. That wetting in the rain has made him bad again."

"Well now I should ask the good Lord to make him strong enough. There's time between this and Easter."

Dudley brightened up at once.

"Do you think he might be strong enough? I should be able to take great care of him, and I would, too. And he's so plucky, that I'm sure the other boys would be good to him."

The cave was reached, and in the interest of watching excavation going on Dudley was soon his bright self again.

He came home radiant, with a match-box full of tiny shells for Roy who was waiting for him in the nursery.

"You have been away a time," he said, wearily: "I'm sure I'm well enough to go out now. I can't bear the winter. It means so many colds and aches."

"Well, you're going to get better very soon, and look here, old chap! If you try your very best, perhaps the old doctor will give you leave to come to school with me after Easter."

Roy's eyes sparkled at the thought.

"Nurse always makes such a molly-coddle of me, and so does granny; but I'll try as hard as I can to be better."

"And now just look at these! Old Principle says these show that the sea must have washed up amongst the hills and into his cave hundreds of years ago, for these belong to salt water fish not river ones. Look at them! 'Fossils' he calls them, they're shells made out of stone. He told me I might give you these from him. I thought he would never go back to his cave again after last December, but he says he feels so much stronger now; and he is very careful how he digs; he won't let me come near him while he does it. And he told me he has been busy writing a paper which he is going to send to some society in London—I forget its name. He is what you call a discoverer, isn't he?"

Roy nodded, then asked anxiously:

"Dudley, were you rude to granny before you went out? Aunt Judy came to look for you here, and she said she hoped you were going to beg granny's pardon for something."

"I'll go now, I had almost forgotten."

And Dudley trotted off to his grandmother's room. She received him sternly, but he was so abjectly penitent that she soon forgave him, and he returned to Roy with a relieved mind.

"It's a dreadful thing to have a temper," he remarked, as he sat upon the nursery table swinging his legs to and fro; "I've given granny an awful headache by the way I banged her door."

"What was it about?" asked Roy, with interest.

"About school," was the answer; "I told her I wasn't going away from you."

"I've been thinking of it a lot," said Roy, with a sigh; "but you'll have to go, and I shall get on pretty well without you. You see a boy with one leg wouldn't be much good amongst a lot of other boys. They would only call him a cripple and push him aside. I shouldn't like them to laugh at me. The only thing for me is a cripple school. Nurse has a little grandson at one. I don't much care for cripples, those I've seen seem very poor creatures with no fun in them, but of course I'm one myself now; only I don't feel like it."

"You're no more a cripple than I am," was Dudley's indignant rejoinder, "why no one would tell anything was the matter with you to look at you."

"We won't talk any more about it," said Roy, "I'm hungry and I hear tea coming."

But both the little hearts were very full of a possible separation, and for some days after it lay like a heavy nightmare on them. Then a letter arrived from Rob which turned the current of their thoughts. It was his first letter from India, and the boys looked at the foreign stamps and paper, as if it were the greatest rarity on earth.

"MY DEAR MASTER ROY:

"I write to tell you we are safely here and I am quite well as I hope you are. It is very hot, but we don't do much work in the middle of the day and I like the place. I wish you could see the flowers and the black men and the funny houses and the colored dresses of the people. I am getting on, I hope, and my sergeant told me the other day I might get the stripe soon if I liked. I will keep a lookout as you told me for Master Dudley's father, but they say India is a bigger place than England, which I don't believe, for we're the grandest nation in the world, and the biggest and the best, all of us in the barrack-room agree to that. I saw a scorpion to-day which pinches when it catches you and draws the blood awful. There is a mountain battery with us now, and they use mules instead of horses, the hills are higher than those at home and it's hard work going up. There is not any fighting yet, but I am ready for it when it comes, and will do my duty to the Queen and you. My chum has helped me write this letter and I hope it pleases you. I am trying to endure hardness. Good-bye, Master Roy,

"Your faithful ROB.

"God bless you."

"That's a much nicer letter, isn't it?" said Roy, in great delight; "that is quite as long as the one I sent him. I hope he will get some fighting soon."

"Supposing if he does, and gets killed?" suggested Dudley.

But Roy put this thought away from him.

"I've known such lots of soldiers in books that come home, that I think he will. Besides God will take care of him. Do you remember the picture gallery at the general's the other day, Dudley?"

"Yes, what about it?"

"I was thinking about that soldier there with all his medals who broke his mother's heart; and then about the soldier boy the general said was the bravest. I suppose I would rather Rob was properly brave like that, than do great things in battle; but I should think he might do both, don't you think so?"

And Dudley nodded, adding, "Rob won't drink or gamble, I'm quite sure."

Amy Le Feuvre

XVI

DAVID AND JONATHAN

Easter came, and to the boys' great delight Roy was so much stronger that it was settled he might accompany Dudley to a private boarding school for one term. Thanks were due to Miss Bertram for this arrangement; and she had great difficulty in obtaining her mother's consent to it.

"I am sure the boys will get on best together; Roy will have a better chance of growing strong if he is with Dudley than if he is to mope by himself here. If we find he does not keep well, we can have him home again; and from all we hear of the school, the boys are most carefully looked after."

And certainly to judge from Roy's appearance and spirits, this plan seemed most successful. It was a bright morning in April. The air was cold but dry, and the old garden was sweet with the scent of hyacinths and narcissuses. Bright beds of tulips and polyanthuses bordered the green lawn, and old Hal was surveying the results of his work with pride and satisfaction. Miss Bertram, in her leather gloves and garden apron, was busy in and out of the hothouses; and the boys, after scampering round in every one's way, had at last scrambled up to their favorite seat on the garden wall.

"This time next week we shall be at school," said Dudley; "how funny we shall feel!"

"We shan't be able to climb walls there, I suppose."

"On half-holidays, perhaps we shall. It isn't all lessons; old Selby told us the happiest time of his life was when he was at school."

"I mean to be happy," said Roy, a smile hovering about his lips.

"And so do I," maintained Dudley, stoutly; "but it will be awfully strange at first. It's like Rob going off to be a soldier. We're going out 'to see life' nurse says."

"Old Principle wants us to come to tea with him before we go. I saw him this morning going past our gate. He'll give us some of his good advice like he did Rob, but I don't mind him, he's such a jolly old chap."

There was silence between them for a few minutes. Dudley was eating a slice of cake which he had brought out of the house with him, and Roy was dreamily watching the figures of his aunt and the old gardener moving about amongst the bright colored flower beds.

"Dudley, we'll always keep friends, won't we?"

"Of course we will."

"But I dare say you'll have a lot of fellows at school who can get about quicker with you than I can; and I don't want to keep you back. I only want you to like me still best in your heart."

"Now look here, old chap! You know that I couldn't like any other fellow better than you. You're much more likely to have a lot of chums than I am, because you're so clever. Look at Rob; he used to think nothing of me at all, and I got to think you didn't want me with you, after he came."

"That was awful rot then, because we two are quite different to any other people. Only it would be a good thing to have a fresh promise together; a kind of Bible covenant, you know, before we go to school."

"All right, here goes, then! Let us have your fists—now then, hear me! I, Dudley Bertram, vow and declare that Fitz Roy Bertram shall continue to be my dearest and nearest chum from this time forth, forevermore. Amen."

Roy grasped Dudley's hands eagerly and earnestly, and repeated his vow in the same words, perhaps with additional emphasis; then with a sigh of relief, he turned to chatter of other things.

Shortly after Miss Bertram came up to them with a newspaper in her hand.

"Granny has just sent out this paper to me, boys. She thought you would like to know that the troops in the place where Rob is, have all been sent out on some expedition against a rebel chief in the mountains, so he will have some fighting now."

"Hurrah!" shouted Dudley, "don't I wish I was with him! Does the newspaper mention his name, Aunt Judy?"

"When shall we have a letter from him?"

"Not for some time yet, because this is telegraphed. It will be all over before we hear. We must hope and pray that Rob may be kept safely through it."

Miss Bertram looked grave, and the boys sobered down at once.

"But, Aunt Judy, of course fighting is dreadful, but it is a soldier's duty, isn't it?"

"And Rob is sure to do his duty."

"Yes, boys, we will hope he will serve his Queen as well as he served us whilst here. Rob was a good boy: I wish there were more like him."

And Miss Bertram moved away, whilst her little nephews worked off their excitement at this news, by jumping down from the wall, and performing a mimic battle in the pine wood outside. Very eagerly and impatiently did they look for a letter before they went off to school, but none came; and the last word that Roy said as he was leaving the house was,—

"Mind, Aunt Judy, you send on my letter when it comes as quick as lightning!"

It was rather an ordeal for both the boys when the last leave-takings of all at home came. The old nurse wept profusely, and was only comforted by the assurance that she should go to her charges on the very first intimation of illness. Mrs. Bertram gave them such warnings against choosing evil companions, and becoming depraved in principles, that the boys were quite awed and depressed; and the servants, one and all, expressed such pity and sympathy for their departure, that Dudley at last confided to Roy:

"If we were going to prison they couldn't look more shocked and gloomy."

General Newton insisted upon taking them himself to school.

"It looks well," he said to Miss Bertram, a little pompously; "for the boys to have a man at their back, and I will have a few words with the principal myself about Roy's delicacy of constitution. It will come with more force from me than from you."

So the general was allowed to have his way, and by the time the boys were in the train with a large packet of sandwiches and cakes to while away the time, their spirits rose, and they declared that going off to school was "the jolliest thing out."

It was late in the evening when they reached their destination. The school was not far from the sea, and the clergyman who kept it would never have more than thirty boarders; his wife, a sweet-faced gentlewoman, received the boys most kindly, and General Newton came away satisfied that it would prove a happy home as well as a good training for the motherless boys.

Dudley and Roy were not long in making themselves at home; their high spirits made them general favorites amongst the boys; and even Roy did not feel himself out of place in the playground, whilst in the schoolroom he proved a quick and intelligent pupil.

"The boys are happy, mother," said Miss Bertram one morning going into her mother's room and handing her two letters; "and Mrs. Hawthorn has written most favorably of them both."

"I should think so," said Mrs. Bertram, stiffly, who though sternness itself to her grandsons was most indignant if any one dared to say a word against them to her; "they would not be true Bertrams if they were not favorites with all."

She opened the letters and read—

"DEAR AUNT JUDY:

"It's our hour for home letters. We like it here awfully. Mrs. Hawthorn is a brick, she lets me come into the drawing-room with her whenever I am tired, but I've only been in once yet because I like to watch the boys play best. I can bowl at cricket and bat too, and I give a boy called 'Gnat' twopence a game to do my runs for me. I'm collecting birds' eggs. There's a boy here who has got 250 of them. I mean to find a sea gull's nest, and then he'll swap twenty of his with me for one gull's, because he has never got one yet. There is a boy called 'Simple Simon,' he thinks I am a wonder because I let him run pins into my cork leg and never cry out. He does not know it's a sham leg and I shan't tell him. We should like another hamper very soon, please. Cook's gingerbread was A1. Give my love to granny, and tell her I take my tonic when I go to bed every night. Give my love to nurse. Tell old Principle Mr. Hawthorn would like to know such a clever man and see his cave. Send me Rob's letter directly it comes, please. We do drill in the gymnasium.

"Your loving nephew

"FITZ ROY BERTRAM."

DEAR AUNT JUDY:

"This is an awfully jolly school. I'd like you to be one of the boys. We are going to have a paper chase next Thursday, and I bet I'll lick some of the chaps at running. Roy and I sleep in the next beds to each other. I look after him when he will let me, he is top of his class and Tom Hunter says he is a plucky chap. Hunter is captain of the eleven. We go to bathe every morning down by the sea, and Hunter says his father is going to give him a boat of his own in the summer. There is a jolly tuck shop in the town. We can go to it every Saturday. There is a boy here called 'Fishy,' he wants to be my chum but I like one called 'Cheshire Cat' better, but I have no chum but Roy. Old Hawthorn only canes for lies. A boy got caned last night, and blubbered like a baby before he went in. I send my love to granny, and all of you. Roy expects Rob's letter every day.

"Your loving nephew

"DUDLEY.

"P.S. Hunter says our cake has made his mouth water for the next."

XVII

ROY'S BIG OPPORTUNITY

"Roy, Mrs. Hawthorn wants you. She has got some letters for you."

Dudley came up excitedly to Roy, directly after dinner was over one Saturday afternoon.

"And I say," he continued; "bring them out and let us go down to the beach to read them together. The tide will be out till the evening."

Roy hastened off, and wondered at Mrs. Hawthorn's grave look.

"Your aunt has sent me some letters to give you, Roy. She has only just received them herself. They are about your friend in India."

"From Rob?" said Roy, with sparkling eyes. "Oh, I thought he never would write. How jolly! And I see his writing, that's my letter."

He held out his hand eagerly but Mrs. Hawthorn laid her hand on his shoulder gently.

Amy Le Feuvre

"Yes, that was a letter he wrote to you before the fighting. Your aunt has heard since—from a nurse who nursed him."

Something in her tone frightened Roy.

"Has he been wounded? He is well again, isn't he?"

"He is quite well now," she said, in a hushed voice.

For a minute Roy gazed at her, with horror and doubt dawning in his dark eyes, then snatching the letters out of her hand he rushed out of the room; and seizing hold of Dudley in the hall he exclaimed almost frantically:

"Dudley, something awful has happened to Rob, let us get away from the house and read these letters."

He held them tightly in his hand, and would not let Dudley take them from his grasp, till they reached the beach.

Then sitting down and leaning against an old weather-beaten rock, Roy, with trembling fingers, first unfolded Rob's letter to himself.

"MY DEAR MASTER ROY:

"We are going up to the mountains to-morrow to fight. The men say it will be stiff work, driving an old chief from his stronghold. Some of them don't like it, but I am ready. I am a better writer now, I hope, so want to tell you what I never have yet. I do thank you with all my heart for being so kind to a homeless lad and taking him in and giving him a happy home. And I thank you much more for teaching him to read and write and giving up your playtime to get him on. But if I was to thank you for a hundred years, I couldn't thank you enough for telling me about my Saviour and showing me the way to heaven. Every word you ever said is sticking to me. I mind all our talks, and if I may have had some rough times in trying to serve God first, I have been as happy as a king. And I have found that the Lord has kept me through the worst times, and I love Him with all my heart. When I get to heaven I shall be able to thank you proper. I do feel thankful to you and Master Dudley. And now good-bye and God bless you.

"Your faithful ROB forever."

Roy read this through.

"He's all right, Dudley. What did she mean? Why did she look so funny?"

Dudley shook his head.

"I don't know, read what Aunt Judy says."

Roy spread out his aunt's letter, and read it in unfaltering tones to the end.

"MY POOR DEAR LITTLE JONATHAN:

"If granny were not really very unwell I should have come straight off to soften the blow to you, but I send the letters which I have just received, and I have asked Mrs. Hawthorn to explain them to you. You must be comforted by knowing that our dear Rob has proved himself a hero and died a hero's death. I know you would like to see the nurse's letter written from the hospital, and I also send you one from the major of his regiment who used to know me years ago. I know you will be a brave boy and bear this trouble like a man. Tell Dudley to write to me by the first post to tell me you have got the letters safely.

"Your loving aunt,

"JULIA BERTRAM."

The letter dropped from Roy's grasp, and he flung himself down on the beach face foremost.

Dudley sat staring out at the sea without speaking. The blow had fallen so heavily, and so unexpectedly, that speech was not forthcoming.

At last Roy looked up.

"You read the other letters to me, Dudley," he said, in a choked voice.

And Dudley, with a good deal of hesitation and effort interrupted by tears, read out as follows:

"DEAR MADAM:

"I have been asked to write to you about Robert White who I am sorry to say was brought into the military hospital the other day dangerously wounded. He lingered three days and was perfectly conscious up to the last. I never saw a braver or more patient lad. He told me all about your goodness to him, and his devotion to a little nephew of yours was most touching. His name was always on his lips. He asked me to tell you the circumstances of his death, and added, 'She will tell Master Roy, I have tried to do my duty. And I will be waiting now in heaven to welcome him. I would have liked to be his servant, but God wants me, and God comes first.' I heard from his sergeant the details of the engagement. A small party of them—White among them—had been ordered to go and take a certain mountain pass, and their officer in command was shot just before they reached it. I wish I could give you the account in the sergeant's own words as he told it me. I will try. 'We were marching up in single file, for the pass was a very narrow one. Through the clefts round it, we saw projecting the enemy's bayonets and spears, and we knew it was certain death for the first one in our ranks. I led the men, and I tell you, Mum, it was a cold-blooded way of meeting one's death, worse than in the fiercest battle fighting shoulder to shoulder! I pulled myself together, tried to say a prayer and marched on, wondering where I should be the next minute, when suddenly before I knew where I was, Corporal White had placed himself in front of me. "You are not ready, sergeant," he said; "I am, let me take your place." It wasn't time to stand arguing, but I tell you I felt queer when I saw the lad stretched for dead under my feet. We had a sharp skirmish, but we drove the enemy back, and the first one I went to look for was White.'

"The sergeant told me this with a sob in his voice; he added that for months he had ridiculed White for his religion and tried to drive it out of him. But he came every morning to the hospital, and I saw him on his knees by White's bedside, offering up a prayer that he might be made a different man.

"And now I must try to give you more details about White himself. I asked him if I could do anything for him the last day he was alive and then he asked me to write to you. He kept the photo of your little nephew under his pillow, and more than once he murmured— 'God first, the Queen next, and then Master Roy—I'll be a faithful servant if I can!' Toward evening I saw he was sinking. I said 'Are you comfortable, corporal?' and he looked up with such a radiant smile: 'Safe in the arms of Jesus,' he murmured, and those were his last words. From what I have heard from those who knew him out here, I gather that his life was a singularly pure and upright one, and that young as he was he had influenced more than one careless drinking man to turn over a new leaf, and be the same as he was. I am forwarding his Bible and small belongings by this mail.

"Believe me, dear madam,

"Yours faithfully,

"ROSE SMITH—Sister in Charge."

Roy listened to this with breathless interest, his eyes shining through his tears.

"Oh, Dudley, how splendid! oh, Rob, you have been a brave soldier, but I shall never, never see you again!"

Down went the little head and a torrent of tears burst forth; whilst Dudley laying his curly head against his cousin's joined him in his weeping. One more letter remained to be read and this was the major's—

"DEAR MISS BERTRAM:

"Having heard from you that one of my men was a

protege of yours, I take the opportunity of saying a word for the poor young fellow. He has been an exemplary character since he came into the regiment, and has, I hear, been a general favorite from his extreme good nature, in spite of being a religious lad. His influence was felt by all his comrades who came in contact with him, and I feel we have lost a smart and promising soldier. The sister in the hospital tells me she is writing particulars of his death. My sergeant is very much cut up over it.

"With kind regards,

"Believe me, yours truly,

"W.A. ALDRIDGE—Major."

"And that's all," said Dudley, mournfully; "why, I can't believe Rob is dead—we never knew he was ill."

Roy took up the letter, and read through Rob's again. Then he looked across the blue ocean in front of him.

"Just read me that bit of the nurse's letter of the fight, Dudley. Can't you think of him marching up to the enemy?"

Dudley read the desired bit, and then with a deep drawn breath Roy said:

"He acted out the song of the drummer boys, didn't he? He marched on to meet his death like they did. I wonder how it felt. Could you have put yourself in front of the sergeant, Dudley?"

"If you had been the sergeant, I could," was the

prompt reply.

"But the sergeant hadn't been kind to him. Oh, Rob, Rob."

"Don't cry so, old chap, you'll make yourself ill. He's happy now. Don't you think we'd better be going in?"

But Roy would not leave the beach till the tea bell sounded, and then he crept in with such a white, weary face that kind Mrs. Hawthorn put him straight to bed, and stayed with him listening to his trouble till tired out and exhausted he fell asleep. When Dudley came to bed he found him clutching the letters tight in one hand, and muttering in his sleep, "God first, the Queen next, and then Master Roy!"

Once in the night he was roused by Roy's grasping hold of his bedclothes.

"Dudley, are you asleep?"

"No," was the sleepy answer, "aren't you well?"

"Yes, but I can't sleep. Tell me, was it my fault? Did I send Rob to his death? I wanted him to go. Did I make him go?"

"Of course you didn't," and Dudley now was wide-awake. "He wanted to go first, and you didn't like it, don't you remember?"

"Yes, I think he liked going; but if he hadn't heard that song perhaps he would never have gone, he would never have wanted to be a soldier."

"He did a lot of good out there. I don't think he will be

sorry now."

Roy settled down to sleep again comforted; but for the next few days he seemed quite unable to give his mind to his lessons, and after some correspondence with Miss Bertram, it was arranged that he and Dudley should go home from Saturday to Monday. It was a sad home-coming, and when Roy saw Rob's Bible his grief burst out afresh. The pages showed how much they had been studied, but no verse was more marked than the one Roy had given him. "Endure hardness as a good soldier of Jesus Christ."

On Sunday evening the boys paid a visit to old Principle. They had been talking about Rob, when Roy said wistfully,

"Rob used his opportunity when he got it, didn't he? I expect he didn't know what a hero he was. I wonder if I shall ever get one come to me. I should like to do something great for God, and great for my country. I shall never give up wishing for a great opportunity to come to me!"

Then old Principle spoke, and his tone was very solemn:

"'Tis not I that will make you proud and uplifted, laddie, but you have been given the grandest opportunity that ever a poor mortal could be given, and you've taken it and made use of it, thank the Lord!"

Both boys gazed up at him with open eyes and mouths.

Dudley said after a minute's thought:

"We've both had some little opportunities, and Roy has

Amy Le Feuvre

had the biggest. He saved me from drowning, and he went into the cave to fetch you!"

"Those weren't proper opportunities," muttered Roy in scorn, "they aren't worth remembering; not after what Rob has done."

"Yes, the opportunity I'm talking of was a grander one than them, though old Principle can't forget he owes his life perhaps to both of you boys' thought of him. 'Tis what the Lord Himself left His throne in heaven for," the old man proceeded in the same solemn tones; "'tis the one thing, the only thing we're told brings joy to the happy ones above; nay to the Almighty Himself, and 'tis wonderful that He will let us have the part in it we do!"

"What do you mean?" questioned Roy awed and puzzled by old Principle's manner.

"I mean this, laddie, you had an opportunity of leading an ignorant soul to the feet of his Saviour; of enlisting a soldier not only in the Queen's service but in the service of the King of Kings; of being the means of filling an empty barren soul with a flood of light and gladness; and of sending out a missionary in the midst of ungodliness and vice, to turn many from the error of their ways. Is it not a greater honor to help to save a soul from destruction, than bring glory to yourself by some feat of physical strength or skill? Thank the Lord on your knees to-night, that He sent you the opportunity you were always hankering after; and thank Him He gave you the grace to seize hold of it, and make use of it for His Glory, not your own!"

Old Principle's burst of eloquence almost startled the boys, and they received it in silence; but later on, as they were walking home in the cool of the evening Roy linked his arm in Dudley's and said softly—

"I see it all now. My broken leg and everything. It was when I was too weak to go out with you, that Rob and I used to talk over these things."

And Dudley replied, with an emphatic nod, "Yes, though you didn't know it, Rob was your big opportunity."

FINIS

Amy Le Feuvre

Choose from Thousands of 1stWorldLibrary Classics By

A. M. Barnard
Ada Leverson
Adolphus William Ward
Aesop
Agatha Christie
Alexander Aaronsohn
Alexander Kielland
Alexandre Dumas
Alfred Gatty
Alfred Ollivant
Alice Duer Miller
Alice Turner Curtis
Alice Dunbar
Allen Chapman
Alleyne Ireland
Ambrose Bierce
Amelia E. Barr
Amory H. Bradford
Andrew Lang
Andrew McFarland Davis
Andy Adams
Angela Brazil
Anna Alice Chapin
Anna Sewell
Annie Besant
Annie Hamilton Donnell
Annie Payson Call
Annie Roe Carr
Annonaymous
Anton Chekhov
Archibald Lee Fletcher
Arnold Bennett
Arthur C. Benson
Arthur Conan Doyle
Arthur M. Winfield
Arthur Ransome
Arthur Schnitzler
Arthur Train
Atticus
B.H. Baden-Powell
B. M. Bower
B. C. Chatterjee
Baroness Emmuska Orczy
Baroness Orczy
Basil King
Bayard Taylor
Ben Macomber
Bertha Muzzy Bower
Bjornstjerne Bjornson

Booth Tarkington
Boyd Cable
Bram Stoker
C. Collodi
C. E. Orr
C. M. Ingleby
Carolyn Wells
Catherine Parr Traill
Charles A. Eastman
Charles Amory Beach
Charles Dickens
Charles Dudley Warner
Charles Farrar Browne
Charles Ives
Charles Kingsley
Charles Klein
Charles Hanson Towne
Charles Lathrop Pack
Charles Romyn Dake
Charles Whibley
Charles Willing Beale
Charlotte M. Braeme
Charlotte M. Yonge
Charlotte Perkins Stetson
Clair W. Hayes
Clarence Day Jr.
Clarence E. Mulford
Clemence Housman
Confucius
Coningsby Dawson
Cornelis DeWitt Wilcox
Cyril Burleigh
D. H. Lawrence
Daniel Defoe
David Garnett
Dinah Craik
Don Carlos Janes
Donald Keyhoe
Dorothy Kilner
Dougan Clark
Douglas Fairbanks
E. Nesbit
E. P. Roe
E. Phillips Oppenheim
E. S. Brooks
Earl Barnes
Edgar Rice Burroughs
Edith Van Dyne
Edith Wharton

Edward Everett Hale
Edward J. O'Biren
Edward S. Ellis
Edwin L. Arnold
Eleanor Atkins
Eleanor Hallowell Abbott
Eliot Gregory
Elizabeth Gaskell
Elizabeth McCracken
Elizabeth Von Arnim
Ellem Key
Emerson Hough
Emilie F. Carlen
Emily Bronte
Emily Dickinson
Enid Bagnold
Enilor Macartney Lane
Erasmus W. Jones
Ernie Howard Pie
Ethel May Dell
Ethel Turner
Ethel Watts Mumford
Eugene Sue
Eugenie Foa
Eugene Wood
Eustace Hale Ball
Evelyn Everett-green
Everard Cotes
F. H. Cheley
F. J. Cross
F. Marion Crawford
Fannie E. Newberry
Federick Austin Ogg
Ferdinand Ossendowski
Fergus Hume
Florence A. Kilpatrick
Fremont B. Deering
Francis Bacon
Francis Darwin
Frances Hodgson Burnett
Frances Parkinson Keyes
Frank Gee Patchin
Frank Harris
Frank Jewett Mather
Frank L. Packard
Frank V. Webster
Frederic Stewart Isham
Frederick Trevor Hill
Frederick Winslow Taylor

Friedrich Kerst	Hayden Carruth	James Branch Cabell
Friedrich Nietzsche	Helent Hunt Jackson	James DeMille
Fyodor Dostoyevsky	Helen Nicolay	James Joyce
G.A. Henty	Hendrik Conscience	James Lane Allen
G.K. Chesterton	Hendy David Thoreau	James Lane Allen
Gabrielle E. Jackson	Henri Barbusse	James Oliver Curwood
Garrett P. Serviss	Henrik Ibsen	James Oppenheim
Gaston Leroux	Henry Adams	James Otis
George A. Warren	Henry Ford	James R. Driscoll
George Ade	Henry Frost	Jane Abbott
Geroge Bernard Shaw	Henry James	Jane Austen
George Cary Eggleston	Henry Jones Ford	Jane L. Stewart
George Durston	Henry Seton Merriman	Janet Aldridge
George Ebers	Henry W Longfellow	Jens Peter Jacobsen
George Eliot	Herbert A. Giles	Jerome K. Jerome
George Gissing	Herbert Carter	Jessie Graham Flower
George MacDonald	Herbert N. Casson	John Buchan
George Meredith	Herman Hesse	John Burroughs
George Orwell	Hildegard G. Frey	John Cournos
George Sylvester Viereck	Homer	John F. Kennedy
George Tucker	Honore De Balzac	John Gay
George W. Cable	Horace B. Day	John Glasworthy
George Wharton James	Horace Walpole	John Habberton
Gertrude Atherton	Horatio Alger Jr.	John Joy Bell
Gordon Casserly	Howard Pyle	John Kendrick Bangs
Grace E. King	Howard R. Garis	John Milton
Grace Gallatin	Hugh Lofting	John Philip Sousa
Grace Greenwood	Hugh Walpole	John Taintor Foote
Grant Allen	Humphry Ward	Jonas Lauritz Idemil Lie
Guillermo A. Sherwell	Ian Maclaren	Jonathan Swift
Gulielma Zollinger	Inez Haynes Gillmore	Joseph A. Altsheler
Gustav Flaubert	Irving Bacheller	Joseph Carey
H. A. Cody	Isabel Cecilia Williams	Joseph Conrad
H. B. Irving	Isabel Hornibrook	Joseph E. Badger Jr
H. C. Bailey	Israel Abrahams	Joseph Hergesheimer
H. G. Wells	Ivan Turgenev	Joseph Jacobs
H. H. Munro	J. G.Austin	Jules Vernes
H. Irving Hancock	J. Henri Fabre	Julian Hawthrone
H. R. Naylor	J. M. Barrie	Julie A Lippmann
H. Rider Haggard	J. M. Walsh	Justin Huntly McCarthy
H. W. C. Davis	J. Macdonald Oxley	Kakuzo Okakura
Haldeman Julius	J. R. Miller	Karle Wilson Baker
Hall Caine	J. S. Fletcher	Kate Chopin
Hamilton Wright Mabie	J. S. Knowles	Kenneth Grahame
Hans Christian Andersen	J. Storer Clouston	Kenneth McGaffey
Harold Avery	J. W. Duffield	Kate Langley Bosher
Harold McGrath	Jack London	Kate Langley Bosher
Harriet Beecher Stowe	Jacob Abbott	Katherine Cecil Thurston
Harry Castlemon	James Allen	Katherine Stokes
Harry Coghill	James Andrews	L. A. Abbot
Harry Houidini	James Baldwin	L. T. Meade

L. Frank Baum
Latta Griswold
Laura Dent Crane
Laura Lee Hope
Laurence Housman
Lawrence Beasley
Leo Tolstoy
Leonid Andreyev
Lewis Carroll
Lewis Sperry Chafer
Lilian Bell
Lloyd Osbourne
Louis Hughes
Louis Joseph Vance
Louis Tracy
Louisa May Alcott
Lucy Fitch Perkins
Lucy Maud Montgomery
Luther Benson
Lydia Miller Middleton
Lyndon Orr
M. Corvus
M. H. Adams
Margaret E. Sangster
Margret Howth
Margaret Vandercook
Margaret W. Hungerford
Margret Penrose
Maria Edgeworth
Maria Thompson Daviess
Mariano Azuela
Marion Polk Angellotti
Mark Overton
Mark Twain
Mary Austin
Mary Catherine Crowley
Mary Cole
Mary Hastings Bradley
Mary Roberts Rinehart
Mary Rowlandson
M. Wollstonecraft Shelley
Maud Lindsay
Max Beerbohm
Myra Kelly
Nathaniel Hawthrone
Nicolo Machiavelli
O. F. Walton
Oscar Wilde
Owen Johnson
P.G. Wodehouse
Paul and Mabel Thorne

Paul G. Tomlinson
Paul Severing
Percy Brebner
Percy Keese Fitzhugh
Peter B. Kyne
Plato
Quincy Allen
R. Derby Holmes
R. L. Stevenson
R. S. Ball
Rabindranath Tagore
Rahul Alvares
Ralph Bonehill
Ralph Henry Barbour
Ralph Victor
Ralph Waldo Emmerson
Rene Descartes
Ray Cummings
Rex Beach
Rex E. Beach
Richard Harding Davis
Richard Jefferies
Richard Le Gallienne
Robert Barr
Robert Frost
Robert Gordon Anderson
Robert L. Drake
Robert Lansing
Robert Lynd
Robert Michael Ballantyne
Robert W. Chambers
Rosa Nouchette Carey
Rudyard Kipling
Saint Augustine
Samuel B. Allison
Samuel Hopkins Adams
Sarah Bernhardt
Sarah C. Hallowell
Selma Lagerlof
Sherwood Anderson
Sigmund Freud
Standish O'Grady
Stanley Weyman
Stella Benson
Stella M. Francis
Stephen Crane
Stewart Edward White
Stijn Streuvels
Swami Abhedananda
Swami Parmananda
T. S. Ackland

T. S. Arthur
The Princess Der Ling
Thomas A. Janvier
Thomas A Kempis
Thomas Anderton
Thomas Bailey Aldrich
Thomas Bulfinch
Thomas De Quincey
Thomas Dixon
Thomas H. Huxley
Thomas Hardy
Thomas More
Thornton W. Burgess
U. S. Grant
Upton Sinclair
Valentine Williams
Various Authors
Vaughan Kester
Victor Appleton
Victor G. Durham
Victoria Cross
Virginia Woolf
Wadsworth Camp
Walter Camp
Walter Scott
Washington Irving
Wilbur Lawton
Wilkie Collins
Willa Cather
Willard F. Baker
William Dean Howells
William le Queux
W. Makepeace Thackeray
William W. Walter
William Shakespeare
Winston Churchill
Yei Theodora Ozaki
Yogi Ramacharaka
Young E. Allison
Zane Grey

www.ingramcontent.com/pod-product-compliance
Lightning Source LLC
Chambersburg PA
CBHW051823170626
46807CB00003B/997